Orbital Claims Adjuster

Adventures of a Jump Space Accountant

Book 2

Andrew Moriarty

ISBN 9781093306644

TO KRIS.

CONTENTS

ACKNOWLEDGMENTS

Special thanks to my wife Kris for putting up with my screaming out loud while I'm editing. I'm sorry I frightened the dog. Thanks to my beta readers Alex, Scott, Vince, and Brian. Thank you for your service guys, and additional thanks to you for pointing out plot holes large enough to drive a truck through. A big truck.

I promise someday I will learn how to spell. Maybe.

PRELUDE

"Shoot me," the sergeant said.

"What?" Jake asked.

The sergeant thrust the shotgun at him. "I said, shoot me."

"Sir?"

"Don't call me sir, I work for a living. Don't worry, I'll load it for you. Watch." The sergeant racked the shotgun, and Jake heard a clacking sound as it chambered a round.

"Trigger's here," the sergeant said, holding the gun up and pointing with his finger. "Point it right here," the sergeant banged his breastplate with his free hand, "and pull the trigger. It'll fire right away."

The sergeant was short and stocky with a disgruntled expression like a pugnacious fireplug. He wore a standard Militia suit—a body-hugging, airtight stocking with inset titanium panels, magnetic boots, hard collars at the wrists and neck for helmet and gloves, and a two-hour atmo-pack on the back. His breastplate read "SGT Russell."

"Are you deaf as well as stupid? Shoot me, I said."

Jake contemplated the gun in front of him. Was this a trick? He'd never shot anything before, except for a shotgun. That had caused him a lot of trouble. But the sergeant seemed set on him doing it. It must be part of the

1

training. Jake stretched his hand forward, then stopped.

"Haven't you ever seen a gun before? Do you even know what this is?" the sergeant asked.

A quiz. Okay. Jake was good at quizzes.

"It's a model 27 boarding shotgun. Holds six shots, weighs 2 kilograms. Chemical propulsion. Shoots in atmosphere or vacuum," Jake said.

Sergeant Russell blinked his eyes. Jake took that as interest and continued. "It's designed for station security troops. Short barrel, 1.2 meters. Easy to store in a model 275 storage container. Low maintenance. Few moving parts. All steel, so it won't rust or vacuum-weld." Jake pointed at the barrel. "That orange-colored barrel and black stock means it's an Old Empire model. The ones printed on Delta have a red barrel. Shortage of pigment for the printers. In fact, many items printed on Delta, even though identical to Old Empire models, have different colors. Delta has a full line of standard pigments, but the more exotic ones are only available if the minerals are sourced locally." The sergeant blinked again. Jake continued.

"Cobalt blue, for example, is only prevalent when there is a major cobalt strike in the Belt. Orange and some other colors require titanium, which is difficult to find."

"Thank you very much, professor," Sergeant Russell said. "But I'm not interested in whether the color of the gun matches your kerchief or your lacy panties. I'm interested in whether you can shoot it. Now shut up and shoot me."

Jake gulped and looked down at the gun. Was this a setup? He didn't want to look like an idiot, not on his first day. Probably as soon as the sergeant gave him the gun he'd beat him up and take it back. Things like that had happened before. Then he'd mock Jake. That had also happened before.

Jake withdrew his hand. The sergeant didn't move his arm, just tilted his head and frowned at Jake.

Jake didn't really want to hurt anybody, but he needed to pass training. But did he really have to shoot somebody to do it? If that was the case, he figured he'd better take the gun and get it over with.

Jake extended his hand again. The sergeant's gun arm didn't quaver. Impressive, given the weight of a fully loaded shotgun. Jake stopped his hand a half inch from the gun. All he had to do was close his fingers and grasp the barrel. But then what? He didn't know how to shoot. He'd never hit anything, never hit a person. What if he screwed up? What if he looked like a fool?

"Make up your mind," Sergeant Russell said.

Jake started to reply but stopped as the side door clanged open. Jake and the sergeant turned to see what was going on.

A short man in a Militia uniform marched in. He walked with the shuffling glide that characterized somebody experienced in low G. When Jake walked, he walked the same way. Behind him were a young man and woman who were bouncing a bit as they moved. Jake assumed they were groundsiders who didn't know how to walk in low gravity. He revised his opinion a bit when he realized the pair were loosely shackled with ankle chains and handcuffs. That was bound to make walking more difficult, no matter the gravity.

The escort walked over to the sergeant, and the shackled pair went to stand beside Jake. The escort extended a data pad to the sergeant, and the two Militia members began a low-voiced discussion.

The new man turned to Jake and extended his hand, at least as far as he could, given it was chained to his ankles.

"Zeke LaFleur. This is my sister, Suzanne."

"Jake Stewart," Jake said, shaking the proffered hand.

Zeke was taller, about 195 centimeters to Jake's 180, and Suzanne was shorter, about shoulder-height to Jake. Both were slim and blond with blue eyes. They both looked athletic in that long-muscled sort of way. Probably runners, since they came from gravity.

"Pleased to meet you, Jake Stewart. Are you from this station?"

"No. I'm from the Belt."

"Really? You are the first Belter we have ever met. Of course, this is our first time on a station."

"I figured," Jake said. Zeke was acting like somebody who had arrived at a cocktail party in a custom spaceship, not dragged into a gym in chains by the Militia.

"Yes? Of course, it must show. We do not walk correctly. The low gravity is difficult for us."

"And we stand wrong," said Suzanne. She smiled at Jake. "We see the others. They slide, but we seem to bounce off the ground and hit things." She spoke slowly and carefully, as if Standard was not her first language, but she had no trace of an accent.

"Just try to keep your feet on the ground and don't push up, push more forward," Jake said.

"Is it hard to learn?" Zeke said.

"I don't think so," Jake said.

"How long did it take you to learn to walk like this?" Suzanne asked.

"I've always known," Jake said. "I grew up on a station."

"Of course. You are lucky to have spent so much time in space, but now my brother and I will be in space as well." Suzanne grinned again at her brother, who grinned back. "We will learn," she said.

Jake shook his head. These were the happiest criminals he had ever met.

The sergeant finished his conversation and pointed at the LaFleurs. The short Militia agent nodded and came over. He began to unlock the leg irons and cuffs. He wasn't gentle about it, and both Suzanne and Zeke had scrapes when he was done. He stepped back and smirked at both of them. "Enjoy your new assignment," he said and shuffled out. Suzanne glared at his back, then turned to her brother. Zeke gave an elaborate shrug.

Aha, thought Jake. They must be descended from Old Empire Francais. The shrug was a giveaway, and it explained the careful phrasing. Francais corporations had been part of the coalition that supported the Old Empire from the start. For hundreds of years after the founding wars, many emperors spoke Francais as a first language, and English and Hindi as a second. Many Delta corporations traced their lineage back to before the empire existed, and traces of their pre-imperial culture still lingered. As recently as fifty years ago, a lot of high-level business was still conducted in Francais. Of course, the abandonment had changed all that. English was now the standard language on Delta.

"Right," Sergeant Russell said. He stepped in front of the three of them and extended the shotgun again. "Back to work. Somebody shoot me."

Zeke's brow furrowed, and he looked at his sister. It was her turn to shrug.

"None of you have the guts? Shoot me!" Sergeant Russell pushed the shotgun farther forward. "You, Stewart. Shoot me."

Jake looked at the shotgun, carefully put his hands behind his back, then shook his head.

"Ask Zeke," said Jake.

"I didn't ask Zeke. I asked you."

"Well. . . ."

"Never mind. Stewart, you're a pussy." Sergeant Russell glared at Jake for a moment, then turned to the others. "This punk won't shoot me. What about you, girl?" He stepped toward Suzanne and brandished the shotgun. "How about it? Want to shoot a Militia sergeant?"

Suzanne stopped rubbing her wrists and nodded enthusiastically. "I would very much like to shoot somebody. You will do." She reached toward the shotgun and looked up at the sergeant. Then she frowned and put her hands on her hips. "This is a setup. It is not loaded.

You will charge us. I am in enough trouble already. You will send us to the south continent."

The sergeant laughed. "You think this is a setup? Watch this." He braced his legs on the floor, pointed the shotgun up at the roof, and pulled the trigger.

BANG! The shot smacked into the ceiling and exploded. Dust and metal pieces drifted down from the ceiling plate. The ejected shell arced lazily up in the low gravity. The tinkle of it hitting the metal floor came a good second after the gunshot blast.

"Does this sound like a setup to you? I, Sergeant Scott Russell of the Delta Militia, order you to shoot me in the chest with this shotgun. Is that good enough for you, LaFleur?"

Zeke spoke up. "Good enough for me. Give me the gun."

The sergeant laughed. "Here," he extended the gun. "Give it your best shot."

Zeke took the shotgun and checked it. He ratcheted it once, loading another round.

"Used one before, have you, kid? Think you know what you're doing?" taunted the sergeant.

"I know what I am doing," Zeke said. He smiled. "But if you want me to prove it, I will show you." Then he frowned. "Sergeant, are you sure you want me to do this? I have nothing against you. Why should I hurt you?"

"Because I told you to, wimp. Come on, too scared?"

"No. Just confused. Okay, sergeant, where do you want to be shot?"

The sergeant expanded his chest. "Give it to me right here, kid." He banged his chest. "Fire away." He leaned back and braced himself.

Zeke shrugged and aimed the shotgun at the sergeant's chest. "Huh. I might like this job." He pulled the trigger.

The shotgun fired. Jake had heard that pellets spread out, that you didn't have to aim a shotgun as much as point it in the general direction. Like a lot of rumors, it was false. The shot only spread a few centimeters over the short distance.

The shot pranged onto the sergeant's breastplate and exploded in a cloud of dust. The shot was frangible—it collapsed as it hit the breastplate. The sergeant absorbed the momentum with a grunt and a flex of his arms. He staggered back but kept on his feet. Jake was impressed. Suits were stiffened with metal to protect the wearer against accidents. Apparently, titanium worked on gunfire as well.

TGI central was a space station. A big one. If they had been on the outermost edge of the cylinder, they would have had nearly .5 G. Zeke could have braced against that. But they weren't at the edge of the station, they were near the core, where the gravity was weak.

Jake had lived in space his whole life. He knew this. But the LaFleurs clearly didn't. Zeke had obviously fired a shotgun before, as he had braced it with both arms, expecting to absorb the recoil. But this was low G. When he pulled the trigger, he didn't absorb the recoil. Instead, he flew off the ground, backwards, and smashed into the wall headfirst. His eyes rolled up as he slid down to the ground. The shotgun dropped from his fingers and clattered to the floor.

"Welcome, everyone, to day one of your Militia spaceman basic," Sergeant Russell said.

1

"All rise for the loyalty oath to the Emperor," said the chairman. The sound system boomed his voice throughout the boardroom. The chairman was thin and bent, with skin spotted by age. He placed both hands on the wooden conference table and shoved his chair back. Then he leaned forward and slowly pushed himself up. An aide stepped beside him and placed a stout wooden cane into his left hand, and then helped lever him up. The chairman leaned heavily on the cane but was able to extract his right hand from the table and pivot to face the stylized representation of Polaris as seen from Earth—three eight-pointed stars, one very large with two smaller ones above it. The imperial emblem.

The meeting table was a wooden oval that seated thirty-seven. The chairman sat at the head, below the imperial emblem. Members of the board faced each other across the table, with chairs for subordinates and specialists against the wall behind them.

The public sat in an elevated gallery that circled three-quarters of the way around the table.

Mr. Dashi rose from his seat in the gallery and faced the imperial seal. He placed his right hand over his heart as he waited for the oath to complete. He flicked his eyes over the board members to see who did likewise. In Delta's constantly shifting political alliances, subtle gestures made big differences. Some members of the council didn't copy the hand movement. He noted who they were and who they worked for.

"I pledge allegiance to the heirs and successors of Emperor Prahmeet IV, last known emperor," he repeated, then sat down with the crowd. The gallery was nearly empty, and he sat alone, with nobody in the same row or the one above or below.

The chairman dropped his hands to the desk, pushed the cane aside, and collapsed into his chair. His well-trained aide grabbed the falling cane and adroitly pushed the chairman's chair underneath him. What should have been a fall turned into a well-rehearsed movement, like a stylized fight in a play.

"The annual meeting of the Emergency Committee of Combined Imperial Control, doing business as the Delta Corporation, is in session," said the chairman. "This is the eighty-sixth extraordinary meeting of the Delta Corporation since the abandonment." He paused to take a sip of water from a glass in front of him. "Motion to accept the minutes of the last meeting. All in favor?" he asked.

The board members sounded bored. "Aye."

"All opposed." Silence.

"Motion carried. Reports," said the chairman. "Communications," he said, turning to a woman seated with a group at the foot of the table.

The woman stood up. She wore what looked like a plain leotard, but cuff, ankle, and collar fittings identified it as a space skinsuit. Four white squares gleamed on her collar. "The Militia reports that we have received no communications from the empire, imperial officers, or forces since the last meeting." She sat down.

The chairman didn't even look up. "Ecology," he said.

A man in the same group as the communications woman stood up. He wore boots and tights. His boots were elaborately tooled. His shirt was loose fitting and hung below his hips, cinched by a tooled leather belt at his waist. It had a stylized collar with four blue and white checkered squares. "The university is pleased to report that we continue on track for terraforming. Planetary average temperature rose .1 degrees this year. We predict similar growth next year. Currently, we are 26.4 percent of the way to our terraforming goal. We anticipate full terraforming in 126.3 years."

A person slid into the chair next to Mr. Dashi. Dashi jumped as a hand poked his leg, then smiled as he turned.

"Hello, Beth."

"Hello, Dashi. Enjoying the show?"

Mr. Dashi was small, bald, brown, round, and neat. Beth was the same height as him, very pale, with an angular face. He was dressed in dark skinsuit, like the presenter, with a dark sash over his shoulder. She wore a calf-length women's dress. Dashi had four red squares on his collar, while Beth had four blue.

Dashi smiled a bright smile at her. "Not much of a show. It's the same every year."

Beth smiled back. "You know that all the important work goes on in committee. All the resolutions are agreed ahead of time. Why do you bother to shuttle down from your orbital sector directory to see this?"

"I like the tradition. The pomp. The politics. The weather. Why do you rail in from your regional directory to see this?"

"The weather. I like that. Politics. There are lots of people here I need to see. Mr. Chairman continues to refuse to die, but he can't put that off forever. There will be a new chairman, a new board member, and new vice presidents and presidents."

"And you want to make sure the allied corporations know what job you want, and what they will get if they vote their shares to vote you in."

"I'm not making promises. I'm just having political discussions, like we are now."

"So, I'm just a political discussion now, am I?"

Beth patted his leg again. "It's always good to see you, Dashi. I missed you."

Dashi smiled. He had known Beth since they were students in university together. They had been briefly involved, until Beth had gone to work for Horizon Construction on-planet, and Dashi had moved on to mostly orbital work. They didn't see each other all year, and only met back up at these meetings. That was enough.

Beth continued. "I want to see how things play out at the top. Who knows, in a few years, I might be in line for a board member spot."

"True. You did come second in finance your graduating year."

"You're an ass, Dashi."

Dashi smiled at her again. He had come first. "You only slept with me because you thought it might throw me off my game for finals."

"Why can't a girl mix work and pleasure?"

"No reason. Why are you really here?"

"Why are you really here?" she said.

Dashi looked around. They were in an isolated bubble of seats. They could talk freely.

"Swap?"

"Yes."

"I want to see the Militia budget, and see what debate happens. My sources tell me they will have to lay up two cutters this year."

"Two cutters? Laid up? Why?"

"They can't do patrols anymore. Fusion plants are too inefficient. They can't run propulsion and life support at the same time. Never mind electronics and weapons."

"But two at once? What will people say?"

"They might not say anything. They might not know.

11

The Militia might just put them in parking orbit near the stations and not tell anybody."

"But people will figure that out."

"Will they? What if they continue appointing captains and crews to them, but they never move? They just hide them in the paperwork. Unless you're watching closely, you'll never realize that those two never go on patrol."

"Interesting. Can't they fix them?"

"The superconductors are getting old. They can be refurbished, but that takes production capacity. There are only so many factories for parts."

"Interesting."

"Your turn."

Beth also paused and looked around. This conversation was unplanned, and they were unlikely to be targeted.

"The monorail is shutting down a station out west. Not enough traffic, they say."

"Really?"

"No. There's plenty of traffic. We need the parts. We're going to disassemble the rails and use them for spares on the main line."

"Why?"

"Same problem with the ships. Old Empire technology is failing. Slowly, but failing. We can make more, but not fast enough. And we're having some problems with resource allocation."

"Resource allocation? That wasn't mentioned in the reports."

"Yes, it was all done in committee. We threatened to remove some items from the shared resource pool if we didn't get more of what we want. We weren't the only ones."

"Huh. What about the corporations out west?"

"There is no single predominant one out there, just bits and pieces of various food companies. And buffalo farms. The executives don't care about the price of buffalo, but the price of regular food could be a problem."

"Will it go up?"

"Hard to tell. They might subsidize it."

Dashi drummed his fingers on his chair arm. "The food from out west is only the higher-priced trays. They'll keep the red, green, and blue trays the same price and push the prices on the higher trays. That's what I'd do."

Beth smiled at him. "That's why I like to talk to you. You always know the answers in advance. Tell me, how do you do that?"

Dashi ignored the question. "It's the only logical solution. Keeps the poor people happy, and the upper class can pay a credit or ten more for a meal."

"For now. But it won't engender support."

"It's the only logical thing to do, Beth."

"People don't always follow logic, especially if you start taking away their privileges. And you never answered how you knew about the Militia thing."

"I never did."

Beth smiled and patted his leg again. "You are a close one, Dashi. Everybody always underestimates you. Except me. I think that's why we get along. What will the Militia do?"

"Hide it. They won't mention the ships being docked. They'll just lie and say their patrol strength is unchanged. That way, the current group of officers can retire and dump the problem on the next generation of leaders."

"The next generation. Meaning us?"

"Meaning us," said Dashi.

The annual meeting limped along. Reports were presented and posted on the net. Formal resolutions that were identical to last year's formal resolutions were adopted. Galactic Growing had lost a two-person courier ship in the far outer rings. The crew's last daily status report said they were all down with some sort of flu but looking forward to a good night's sleep before their final burn to bring them back in-system. They never made the final burn and didn't communicate again. Maneuvering thruster failure in the Militia was up 24 percent, but replacements were adequate. Fusion plants had dropped .5 percent in efficiency across the fleet. Consumption of carrots was down 13 percent. The price of fish was down 30 percent.

Finally, the chairman banged his gavel and closed the meeting. Everyone shook hands and went home. Dashi hugged Beth before she left to mingle on her own personal journey of self-aggrandizement. He felt a bit sad. They were still friends, but he could see a time soon when they would become rivals and eventually enemies.

He turned down the offer of a drink in a nearby bar from other colleagues and headed back to his hotel to get on the net. All the divisions of the Delta Corporation had to publish annual reports at the same time. Much could be learned from perusing them. And the wired connections on-planet were much faster than the wireless ones in orbit.

Dashi sat down in his hotel room and began to read. The empire was still gone. There were still no jump ships. Trade was reasonable. Nobody was starving. Inflation was almost non-existent. The stock market crept sideways. Corporations still maneuvered for advantage. The population grew slightly. Not enough for concern, but economists' long-term forecasts were not optimistic. The money supply was having problems keeping up. Actually, there would be deflation in prices this year if current trends continued. Unemployment was very low but creeping up slowly. The only mild worry was that some marginal manufacturing plants were to be shut down, a hauler shuttle was decommissioned, and some marginal mines were to be closed. Galactic Growing was going to shut down an orbital nickel mine because the cost of repair parts made it uneconomical. They were also going to decommission one of their industrial-size 3D printers.

All this sounded benign, but Dashi knew there was another side to it. There were no new manufacturing plants being opened. Rebuilding the hauler shuttle was beyond their technological capacity, so it would never be replaced. The deflation was probably going to be permanent, and unemployed people would have to go somewhere, probably right here at landing, which would explain the small groups of younger men and women he saw lounging around during the day.

But Mr. Dashi was more interested in the nickel mine. The system was swimming in nickel from the asteroids, and a little more or less wouldn't make any difference. But nickel wasn't the only thing that that mine produced. The list of byproducts included selenium, ruthenium, and many rare earth minerals. Most of the byproducts were listed not in percentages, but as parts per million. But process enough nickel ore, and the parts per million added up.

Ruthenium, selenium, and platinum group metals were critical materials for the manufacturing of ion thrusters and fusion plant magnetics. And you didn't "decommission" a valuable 3D printer. Those were Old Empire. It must have broken and been unrepairable. That was one less source of high-tech material for the colony.

After about six hours Dashi headed downstairs for a drink. He wanted to go out for a walk and decided to go to the bar his colleagues had invited him to after the meeting. He had just stepped out of the lobby door when hotel security intercepted him.

"Beg pardon, sir, but if you are looking for a drink or a bite to eat, there are some fine places over there," said the uniformed guard, gesturing back across the street from the hotel.

"I was thinking of going downtown to the conference center to meet up with some friends."

"It's a little late for that, sir, and not the best idea to walk down there alone at this time of night. We'd rather you didn't. But if you are set on it, just give us a minute and we'll rustle up a ground car and an escort or two."

"An escort? How dangerous is it down there?"

"Not dangerous at all, sir. Fine place. Very safe. But the

younger folks can get a little rambunctious at night out in the streets. Just blowing off steam, you understand. They would never bother a group of, say, three people. We'll get you a couple of the boys lickety-split, and they'll take you into the center there. We'd be embarrassed if an executive was harassed."

Dashi thanked him courteously for his help, but said he'd changed his plans and walked across the street to the secure bar instead.

He wondered how many unemployed there actually were. If the Militia wasn't reporting the status of its ships accurately, what else wasn't being reported properly?

***

The next morning Dashi took hotel transportation to the shuttle port. His shuttle took its place in the run up to the mass driver. Metal containers loaded with products were put on the kilometer-long track, and superconducting magnets accelerated them to orbital velocity. Dashi buckled in, emptied his pockets, and arranged his legs, arms, and clothes. The shuttle reached up to 4 G for an extended period, and he didn't want a data pad in the wrong place to give him bruises or interrupt blood flow and cause him to pass out. The trans-sonic boost period seemed to take forever, but eventually they were airborne and free-falling. Dashi waited while they floated and thought deeply about magnets and how important they were to Delta and its economy, and how they were manufactured.

"It's beginning," Mr. Dashi said to himself.

2

Jake had graduated from the TGI Merchant's Academy with no fanfare. The other students had finished their exams, had them graded, found out their marks, celebrated, then attended the graduation ceremony accompanied by friends and family. Jake had been unable to attend his exams because he had been kidnapped by a rebel group who had framed him for killing his boss and trying to steal a shipload of weapons. He missed his graduation because he was involved in a firefight in an airlock in TGI main station that led to depressurizing a large part of a loading dock, theft of several hundred old-empire automatic weapons, and the death of his best friend. At least, that was the story.

The reality was somewhat more complicated, and even his new boss, Mr. Dashi, didn't know all of it. But Mr. Dashi had hushed up the more unsavory parts and struck a deal with Jake. If Jake kept his mouth shut, in return for a passing mark and a commission as a Fourth Officer in the TGI Merchant Service, any Militia charges would go away. Jake had agreed to four years of service and "special duty," reporting at all times directly to Mr. Dashi.

Mr. Dashi's position was somewhat nebulous. Jake had

known him as one of his professors and head of the students at the Merchant Academy. It later turned out that he was the second most senior TGI representative in this orbital sector and seemed to be in charge of many other things. He had no difficulty getting Jake transferred and seemed able to have Jake attached to any class or ship that he wanted. Mr. Dashi was well spoken, neat, formal, and polite at all times. He never raised his voice, and smiled often. Jake was scared to death of him.

Jake stood in Mr. Dashi's large office. The walls were covered with wood paneling—incredibly expensive in space—and his furniture appeared to be solid wood. Jake figured he could probably eat for five years on what one of the chairs cost.

"Mr. Stewart. Welcome back. I see you had no trouble with your exams," said Mr. Dashi. He smiled at Jake and twirled his small mustache.

"No sir," answered Jake.

"Not that we expected any." He handed Jake some papers. "Here is your commission, a Fourth Officer in the TGI Merchant Service, Admin Division."

Jake's head came up. "We had talked about the Deck Division, sir."

"We had. Something has come up. Needs of the service. It's necessary for you to be in admin for a time. But I'm not against you cross-training while you work. You are a smart man. You figure things out. When the time is right, we'll transfer you."

Jake frowned. He'd gone to the Merchant Academy to escape scut work at his home station. He'd worked hard to graduate, and Mr. Dashi had offered him a job as a sort of corporate troubleshooter, keeping an eye on things and reporting back to him. Spying, basically. But spying as an officer on a spaceship, not as an administrator.

Jake wanted to be a spy, not an accountant.

"That wasn't in our agreement, sir."

"It wasn't? I thought you read the entire contract

through?"

"I did, sir. Twice."

"Then you're familiar with sub-section G, which outlines 'exigencies regarding necessary changes due to the needs of the service'?"

Jake cursed inwardly. He had read that section. "I just assumed that you would honor the spirit of the arrangement, not the letter, sir."

"You did, Mr. Stewart? As I recall, you twisted your contract with us totally out of shape to allow yourself to attend the academy, never mind graduate."

That was true. "Sir, I did take an aggressive view of what I was entitled to."

"Indeed, as you should. As did I. If you wanted a more formal arrangement, we could have discussed it."

Jake pondered. Since a more formal arrangement might have had him going to jail for murder, he thought that he should change the subject.

"Never mind, sir. It's no shame to be beaten by a master."

"Hardly that, Mr. Stewart. I'm just a simple bureaucrat trying to make the most efficacious use of my resources."

Now Jake was jealous. Mr. Dashi had maneuvered him into doing something he didn't want, and he had also used both the words "exigencies" and "efficacious" within two minutes. Jake wasn't sure he could spell either word, never mind use them properly in a sentence.

"Yes sir."

"You do need more training. If you are going to be in the Admin department, you must be trained to be an administrator. We have you registered in a six-month course on administrative rules and procedures, and following that, six months on cargo handling paperwork. Then you'll be ready to pass your TGI licensing tests."

"Another year in school, sir?"

"Yes."

"I see, sir," Jake said. He paused. Dashi steepled his

fingers in front of him and stared back. Neither said anything for a moment.

"Sir. I don't want to do that," Jake said. "I feel like I've had enough school for now. And cargo handling paperwork is boring."

"You believe it would be boring, Mr. Stewart? I disagree. I enjoyed my year learning administrative procedures immensely."

"Sir, I have another, I think better, solution."

Mr. Dashi unsteepled his fingers and flipped his hands open. "Please share that with me, Mr. Stewart."

"Sir, I don't need to go to school. I can learn this by myself. I've already read the TGI policies and procedures manual. I've done cargo handling all my life. Let me study for these exams on my own. Just a bit of a refresher and I'll be ready to take the tests."

"That's certainly possible. You did well in my class. But what advantage accrues to TGI from this arrangement?"

Accrues? You needed a thesaurus to have a conversation with this guy, Jake thought.

"I'll be able to do field work for TGI while I study. You can send me on other jobs, and I'll study at night and on weekends, or in my free time."

"This sounds not unreasonable," Mr. Dashi said.

"Of course, some benefit should . . . accrue to me as well."

"What type of benefits are you suggesting, Mr. Stewart?"

"I want to go to pilot training, sir. Next class opening, I want it."

"You want to be a pilot, Mr. Stewart?"

"I want to take the training, sir."

"A subtle, but important difference. Very well—I suggest this. No school. You are to take, and pass, the admin level 1 and 2 license exams, and the cargo handling level 1 and level 2 exams within the next six months. Once you have passed both exams, I will get you a slot in the pilot evaluation simulation—the test that we run on our regular pilots every two years to check how up-to-date their training is. I can't guarantee you a spot in a training class without you taking the evaluation, but if you do well in the evaluation, we'll see what we can do. Until that time, we'll assign you to other work as appropriate. Does that sound fair?"

"Yes sir."

"Good. let me explain your first task to you."

The goal, Mr. Dashi explained, was simple. Some of Mr. Dashi's friends had been approached by an executive from another company. He was the general manager of their freight and shipping concerns, and he had a gambling habit. A bad one. He took the shuttle up to the orbitals to gamble every few weeks and lost heavily. Now his debt was due, and he didn't have it. The executive, Colivar, had approached Dashi's friends with an offer to sell his shipping schedules and profit margins for the last five years. These friends contacted Dashi. Dashi was appointing Jake to go and collect some intelligence information.

"Just statistics, really," Mr. Dashi said. "That's one of our main jobs here, in addition to running the school. The school employs a lot of professors, so we have access to specialists in lots of different areas, and we have extensive computing and communication resources. We use that to get an idea of our business competitors' capabilities. We mostly collect raw data from public sources and publish reports. Occasionally, we get offers like this. And if they are good, we take them."

"So, you want me to go buy this information?" Jake asked.

"No, we're not at that stage yet. We were promised a sample. Colivar is going to be at a bar near the shuttle dock tomorrow night at about twenty hours. We'll give you a picture and some information about him. I want you to go to the bar, have a few drinks, blend in. Wait till he comes in. When he does, go sit down with him. Tell him you are there to pick up a data chip he has."

Jake waited to see if there was more. The silence stretched.

"That's it? Isn't there a secret code word or something?"

Mr. Dashi leaned back in his chair, folded his hands, and smiled.

"Mr. Stewart, this isn't a video. He's offered to give us some corporate information. Just go and get it. Bring it back and drop it in the lockbox chute."

"The lockbox?"

"Yes. We'll have somebody look at it the next day. If it's worthwhile, he'll be contacted. If not, we'll just forget it."

"What if he wants to be paid first?"

"If he doesn't want to give it to you, then just leave the bar and go back to your quarters."

Jake blinked for a moment.

"I can do that, sir. But it seems so . . . banal?"

Mr. Dashi laughed. "It's what I need done, Mr. Stewart. Is it too banal for you? Should I find somebody else?"

"Oh, no, sir. I'll do it. I just thought this job would be more exciting."

"I'm sorry we're not living up to your expectations, Mr. Stewart."

"Oh, no, sir. I'm sorry. I can do this."

"Good. Jose will send you the info," Mr. Dashi said.

"Thank you, sir," Jake said.

***

Jose was the most efficient and organized man Jake had ever met. Which explained why he was Mr. Dashi's assistant.

"Information is in your email. Here's a corporate credit chip, for drinks and other needs. Buy a few drinks on it for you and for Mr. Colivar. Congratulations, you are officially on expenses now," Jose said.

"Wowzers." Jake stood still for a moment. He had a corporate credit chip. This was good. "How much can I spend?"

"You can spend what you need. The rules are fairly loose, and Dashi doesn't audit very closely. What does 'wowzers' mean?"

"I saw it in an Old Empire vid. Belters curse too much. So, I can spend what I like? Buy a drink in the bar?"

"If you want. Buy two drinks if you want."

"Can I buy other people drinks?"

"Jake, I'm not going to go through everything for you. You're working for Dashi now, use your discretion. Read a manual. There must be an expense handbook, right?"

"There is. I've read it."

"Of course you have. You're good with rulebooks."

"Yes. Jose, how did you know to have all this information and the credit chip set up for me? Mr. Dashi and I just negotiated this job for me five minutes ago."

"Negotiated? How so?" Jose asked. Jake explained the discussion and the negotiation about the school, and the licenses, and pilot training.

"Jake, let me summarize this 'negotiation' that you just did. You promised Mr. Dashi to do a year's worth of studying in six months, on your own time, while he's free to have you do other work during the day. And in return he's going to let you go to a one-day simulation test that anybody can sign up for, with nothing firm promised even if you pass it?"

"Anybody can sign up?"

"Yep."

"So he hasn't really given me anything, has he?"

"Nope."

"You've had all this info for me for days, haven't you?"

"Yes."

"He manipulated me into asking for it, didn't he?"

"Yep."

"Wowzers. Dashi is good at this."

"Very good. But one more thing."

"Yes?"

"Dashi smiles a lot, but he doesn't like failure. If you want to keep working here, you need to produce results. Don't screw up, or it's back to Rim-237 or whatever dead-end station faster than you can say 'employment terminated.'"

***

Jake had already left by the time Dashi finished reading his notes and punched his intercom.

"Jose, come in please. I have some tasks."

Jose didn't bother to knock, but came right in.

"Sir?"

"Find out everything you can about system production of platinum group metals, particularly ruthenium. And find out how much of that comes from Galactic Growing and where."

"Of course, sir. Public sources only?"

"No, you can use other means. And don't worry about the usual budget. Get me the info as quickly as you can," said Dashi.

***

Jake stepped through the door into the After Burner. As spaceman's bars went, this one was swankier than he was used to. He was several levels down from the cargo docking ports, on the same ring level as the shuttle docking ports. On a station, that made this a better neighborhood. It had chairs, not stools, and there were actual cushions on them.

The bartender had an all-black custom skinsuit on with the bar's logo tastefully displayed in burning yellow on his breast pocket. Two men sitting near the bar wore full-fledged business suits with ties. At first, Jake thought they didn't have skinsuits on at all, which was the height of idiocy on a station, but a closer view showed a very discreet brown fashion suit that blended seamlessly with their skin. Jake had heard of such things, but they were ruinously expensive—it cost a lot to match the wearer's skin tone exactly. Two girls talking at the bar wore colorful headbands, wristbands, and turbans with inset green gems. Probably peridots, thought Jake. They were formed in the core of asteroids. Growing up he had known several Belters who specialized in prospecting for them.

Jake realized he stood out in his Belter semi-hard suit with attached equipment belt. He wasn't really dressed as a corporate operative. Okay, he wasn't actually a full-fledged operative yet. He hadn't been fully trained. He hadn't done much in the way of spy-type things. And by "not much" he meant none. He'd really only gone to classes on TGI's internal accounting system.

Today was his first job. Go to this bar. Buy some drinks. Watch for a contact in the bar. Approach him. Get the data. Report back. Save his receipts. He marched up to the bar.

"What will it be for you, kid, a Belter Beer?" asked the bartender.

"How did you know I'm a Belter?" Jake asked.

"Well, you're carrying a Belter helmet, you have Belter work boots on, a Belter equipment belt, and you also have a Belter accent."

"Oh," Jake said. This spy thing might be more complicated than he thought.

"The boots look solid."

"They were my dad's."

"You wear your dad's boots? Doesn't he need them?"

"He's dead. I inherited them."

"Oh. So, kid, a beer?"

"Um. No." Jake tapped his fingers on the bar and

looked at the displayed bottles. He was going to be a spy, dammit. What did spies order in the vids? "I want something, more . . . sophisticated. What do you have?"

The bartender looked at him skeptically. "A rich Belter? That would be a first."

Jake pulled out his corporate credit chip.

"TGI has me on expenses," Jake said.

The bartender took the card, shrugged, and checked it with his scanner. His eyebrows rose when he saw the company-provided limit. He straightened up and turned back with a smile.

"Mr. Stewart. Welcome to the After Burner. I'm Lorenzo, and I'll be your bartender for tonight. Anything you want, please let me know. The more discerning members of our clientele drink this." He reached under the bar and produced a metal tray covered with a purple satin napkin. With a flourish, he whipped the napkin off.

"Schnapps. From the surface. A special kind," Lorenzo said.

"A special kind?" Jake asked.

"Yes, made from retsina spirit. Try it." The bartender cracked the seal and poured a shot. Jake took a swig of it and nearly gagged. He looked up and saw the bartender knot his forehead and give him a slightly disapproving look. Jake hurriedly drank the rest of the vile liquid and began to cough.

"Smooth," Jake said when he had his breath back.

"Indeed," said the bartender, pouring him another shot. "Free trades, sir."

"Free trades."

Jake shot the second shot and began to cough again.

***

Two men sat in silence in the darkened corner of the After Burner and watched the show Jake was putting on. The corner was dark enough that only their outline could be seen. They were average height, average weight, dark-complexioned, and totally forgettable. They wore stained work coveralls, like a janitor would. It was difficult for them to talk to each other because they sat side-by-side at a table, rather than across from each other. But they were very well placed to observe the entire bar, and only a very astute observer would have noticed that they both had their backs to the wall and that by sitting side-by-side, both could have their weapon hands inside small, revolver-sized bags on their laps.

"That's the new TGI operative?" the first one asked.

"Seems like. He matches the description."

"That kid? Did the description include poorly dressed?"

"We don't normally see much Belter gear here, that's true. He looks like a comedy act—'rich Belter comes to town.'"

"Did he just buy a bottle of that crappy pine tree wine?"

"Yup. Lorenzo distills it and is pushing it as some sort of special schnapps, a surface thing."

"He can't be an operative. He's too young and too stupid."

"Well, we were told that somebody would be here to meet Colivar, and he's clearly TGI."

"He just announced that publicly. How stupid can he be?"

"Pretty stupid, I guess. He's buying Mary a beer for her birthday."

"It was her birthday last week."

"When someone else is buying, it's her birthday every day."

"What's Colivar doing?"

"He's over there. He's not moving."

The second man didn't move his head but tracked the first's man's eyes to the far corner, where a short, red-haired man with a red beard watched the drama at the bar unfold.

"He's not happy. This must be the pickup. Think he'll approach?"

"We can only hope."

"Let's make sure this goes sideways for him, then." The first man stretched in his chair. The movement drew a look from the bartender. The first man nodded, ever so slightly. The bartender nodded in return. He turned away from Jake and reached under the bar, then palmed a small green pill and poured another shot for Jake, crushed the pill between his fingers, and poured the powder into the glass. He waited a second for it to dissolve, then turned around and presented it to Jake.

**

Jake had been joined by not just one, but two girls at the bar. "It's your birthday as well?" he said to the second girl, his speech slurring. He tried to concentrate a bit harder. He was having trouble seeing properly. One was blonde, and one was brunette, but everything else was kind of blurry. This retsina was strong stuff.

"What are the odds?" the bartender asked, delivering a round of beers for the girls and taking the opportunity to pour another round of shots. "Another bottle, sir?" he asked Jake, who nodded assent.

"Actually," slurred Jake, "it's not that unreasonable. People think that the odds are higher than they actually are, but if you take 364 days in a year, there is a one-in-364 chance that two people have the same birthday. But if you start combining them, the chances of it happening in a group of people, you see, you have to start adding the odds together, two-in-364, plus three-in-364. . . ." Jake kept talking. Math was one of his favorite subjects. The girls were attentive. Girls who loved math, wasn't that great! He felt smart. He felt attractive. He felt bulletproof.

The girls kept drinking and smiled at Jake as he talked. Jake racked his brain—wasn't he there to do something else? He couldn't quite remember. Focus—right, he had to meet a guy. In the corner. Red hair, red beard. He turned to look and staggered a bit. He wasn't very coordinated. He banged into a group of four at the bar, jogging their shoulders and spilling their drinks. The lead drinker, an older fellow with gray hair and heavily muscled arms, cursed and turned toward Jake.

"What are you doing, kid?"

"I don't like your attitude," said Jake.

"Son, you better apologize or it's more than my attitude that you won't like."

Jake looked at him for a moment and then cocked his fist and swung. He was a spy, and spies in the vids did things like that.

It was a surprise. The older guy had expected a little more posturing, or for Jake to back down in the face of four-to-one odds. But Jake was too far gone and gave it his best shot. He connected easily with the man's chin, snapping his head backwards. The man staggered but didn't fall.

Jake stared at the old man. Why didn't he fall?

"They always fall in the vids," Jake said. He balled his fists and held them out in front of his face. He'd seen that in vids too.

The old man shook off his surprise and looked at Jake for a second. Then he moved, fast. He weaved left, stepped inside Jake's thrown fist and hit him in the stomach ten times in two seconds, making sure to catch his liver. Jake felt a horrible pain in the lower-right quadrant of his stomach, gasped, and bent forward, clutching his midsection. The old man kneed him in the chin and threw him to the ground, jumped on his chest, and began to hit him in the face. His friends gathered around and began kicking Jake in the ribs and legs.

They had clearly seen different vids than Jake had.

"Hey," yelled Lorenzo. The four men stopped pummeling Jake and looked back. Lorenzo had a shock stick in one hand and a hard phone in the other. "No murders in the bar. Militia are on the way. They'll be here in a few minutes. You can finish him off and be busted, or get."

"And what's to stop us giving you some of this before they get here?" asked one of the men, holding up a fist.

"This," said Lorenzo. He pointed the shock stick in his hand and thumbed the button on the top. A bright blue light arced from the stick to the nearest man's chest. He shook violently under the electric onslaught, then fell face first, smashing his head on the edge of the bar as he fell forward.

The men went.

The red-haired man in the corner shook his head, finished his drink, and walked out the door. The two shooters in the corner looked at each other, shrugged, and followed the redheaded man out.

The Militia patrol arrived, conferred with the bartender, and checked the unconscious man on the floor next to the bar. A call brought a medical team running. They gave Jake a brief once-over and left him, but put the other man on a backboard and raced him out the door. The patrol further conferred with the bartender and then carried Jake's unconscious form out the front door. The bar patrons had all stood up to see what was going on. They retreated back to their tables once the patrol left, conversations buzzing between them.

At a table on the other side of the bar sat a short, balding, chubby man. He was dressed in a scruffy business suit and was drinking the second-cheapest beer on the menu. If you had looked at him more than once, you would have seen an unsuccessful businessman enjoying a beer while he reviewed a densely written contact. But you wouldn't look at him more than once.

Like everybody in the bar, he had stood up to watch

the fight. Under the cover of the noise and confusion, he had carefully slid his hand comm down the table until one end pointed to the shooters. The built-in camera locked on and took a dozen pictures of the two men. He waited until they had left to examine the results. He was especially pleased with the clarity of one shot under a bright light. Between the pictures and his own notes, he was sure he'd be able to identify them again. He returned to his seat as the commotion subsided and waited an extra half hour before carefully packing up his papers. He paid for his drinks with cash, including a moderate tip, and walked quietly out the door.

The two girls had retreated to the far side of the bar, whispering with each other. They flagged the bartender down.

"Where did they take him?" they asked.

"Jail."

"Do you still have his credit chip?"

"Yes."

"He said we could drink on his tab as long as we wanted."

The bartender reached up to the top shelf and pulled down an expensive-looking bottle, cracked the seal, and poured three shots.

"That's what I heard too, ladies."

3

Mr. Dashi sat in his well-appointed office and leaned back in his desk chair. It was a heavy wooden chair that scraped as it rolled over the floor, and Dashi had been forced to run it on bare metal—it destroyed any carpets he put underneath it. The numbers that Jose had collected him for platinum group production from Galactic Growing were surprising. Very surprising. He touched his desk comm.

"Jose, please come in here."

Five seconds later the outer door opened. Jose came in and sat down in one of the carved wooden chairs in front of the desk.

"Sir?" Jose said.

"You predict Galactic Growing will have a 30 percent drop in platinum production, and up to 70 percent of other platinum group metals when they close this nickel mine?"

"Yes sir. They don't actually have any platinum mines per se. It's all a byproduct of their nickel mining. That mine doesn't make any money because of the low price of nickel. Even the higher price for the platinum group metals won't compensate for the losses on the nickel. They believe that the new mine—Rim-171—will fill the gap. But it won't be ready for at least a year. In the meantime, they are trading for the minerals they need to keep their plants running."

"Trading with whom?"

"Free Traders, independent stations . . . there's a list in one of the appendices. They send ships out to do regular trade with their allied corporation stations, and they buy the metals they need as they go by."

"I see. How certain are you of this information?"

"Very certain, sir. I have at least three distinct sources for everything presented in my report."

"Three sources?" Mr. Dashi shook his head. "That's not possible. I only asked you about this, what, a day ago? It takes months or years to develop sources this detailed. I know—I used to have your job."

"Yes, sir, but I didn't so much develop sources as use commerce. I bought internal reports off GG staff."

"Which ones?"

"All of them."

"What? All the staff? Or all the reports?"

"Both, sir."

"How?"

"Well, you see, sir, you did say it was urgent."

"Yes?"

"So, I changed a big bucket of the budget to ready cash, and I hopped a shuttle to Galactic Growing's main station."

"You went to their main station?"

"I did, sir. I went down to their cafe at lunch, and I stopped at every table."

"And did what? Ate thirteen red-green-blue trays till you were too bloated to move?"

"No, sir. I told everybody that I was a spy and that I wanted to buy GG corporate secrets. I said I would pay well, and I would be at the casino next and gave them a card with my contact info."

"You told them you were a spy? You gave them a card?" Jose could tell Mr. Dashi was surprised. It was the first time he hadn't smiled when talking to him.

"Yes, sir. It's a very nice card. Stylish, I think. Would you like one?"

"No, thank you. Wait, yes. No, never mind. You told them you were a spy and that you would pay them to spy on their employer."

"Yes, sir. The traditional way—meeting them quietly, developing things—would take too long. So, I just told everybody where to find me and that I was buying, and I left a lot of those cards around. The only thing I told them was they had only two hours to contact me. That way, they wouldn't have time to fake a report."

"You got reports?"

"Yes, sir. One hundred and forty-seven."

"Jose, now they know we're looking into their mining production."

"No, sir, they don't. I didn't specify what type of reports I was looking for, and I bought pretty much everything that people offered me. Thirteen of them were related to mining. And they were from several different departments so I was able to crosscheck the information. I'm very confident of my numbers. I also know a great deal about their childcare policies."

Mr. Dashi shook his head. It wasn't the traditional way of recruiting spies, but he couldn't argue with the results.

Jose continued. "They already know we spy on them, sir. And I didn't get anything really secret—nothing like strategy or expansion plans, just mundane shipping and production reports. But there were so many of them, I was able to figure a lot out."

Jose began to go over the numbers in more detail. The gist of it was that GG planned to make up for their shortfall by buying platinum group metals on the market until their next mine went into production. They didn't have a single source for the metals. Instead, they had sent their trading ships on routes that covered a lot of marginal stations. These stations were technically affiliated with GG but only saw one or two ships a year, so they were forced to take care of themselves. Since GG only sent one ship a year, if the station wanted to buy or sell anything, they pretty much had to take the prices they were offered, when they were offered. Many of these stations stockpiled a year's production at a time, ready to sell when the annual ship arrived.

Dashi leaned back and steepled his hands in thought. Jose recognized Mr. Dashi's deep-thinking pose and didn't say anything. Eventually, Dashi leaned forward.

"Jose, we need a plan to get as many of these resources for TGI as we can in the next few months, before this shortage makes itself felt. As many as we can, even if we have to stockpile them. Cost is no object. They will be critical for Delta's future prosperity. For TGI's future prosperity as well."

"Yes sir. I figured as much. I have a plan."

"Of course you do. Elaborate."

"We'll send a fast trading ship on the same route that GG is taking and scoop up whatever is available. If we get there first, we can get several years' worth of platinum group metals at a reasonable price."

"I'm not so worried about the price, but I am worried about the quantities."

"With the right ship, we can do that, sir. We just need something fast and with a long range. We'll have to sacrifice cargo space for reaction mass and supplies."

"Will that cause us a problem in storage?"

"No sir. We're talking thousands of kilograms, not tens of thousands. The important stuff will mass pretty low. You could probably put all of the rare earths in a few big transit cases."

"Good. We need as much as possible."

"I'm a little confused about that, sir. May I ask why we need so much?"

"Ruthenium is used to make a variety of things, among them grids for the ion thrusters."

"Yes sir. So, when there's a shortage of ruthenium we can corner the market and sell it to the other corps. Good plan, sir."

Dashi shook his head slowly. "No, I don't think we'll do that. I don't think we'll sell any at all. We're going to keep the metals for ourselves, for our own repairs. Thrusters are only supposed to last so long, and we've already exceeded their designed lifetime. They have started failing in greater numbers. We're going to need those metals for more and more repairs."

"Can't we make new thrusters, sir?"

"We haven't had that capacity since the abandonment. We can refurbish some of our current thrusters, but not all of them. I'd say less than 50 percent. Some are worn beyond repair. And we simply lack the industrial capacity to build new ones. Wrong type of 3D printers."

Jose was very smart. If he wasn't, he wouldn't be Dashi's assistant. He caught on fast. "So, an entire ship could be immobilized by the lack of thruster grids, which means it isn't available to pick up other resources, which means the remaining ships have to do double duty, which means their thrusters will wear out faster. . . ."

Dashi nodded. "Yes, and not just the thrusters—there will be more wear on other ship systems, like the fusion plants, and then things will cascade. It may already be happening. We've used up a lot of the capital goods that were left here after the abandonment. We can't keep going the way we've been. We'll have to settle at a new equilibrium."

"Sir, if we pick up those extra metals, GG won't be very happy with us. There will be consequences."

"Well, I don't want to start a corporate war. Everybody would lose then. But it will be better if one central entity has the capability to allocate the necessary resources."

"One central entity meaning TGI, sir?"

"Of course. Have you picked a ship?"

Jose hesitated. "Yes sir. I have one we can hire. It belongs to one of the allied corps. It's a subsidized far trader, and it would be perfect for this type of work. It comes with a full crew, and we even have some TGI contractors on board. The problem is which contractors."

"Who is it?"

"Bassi Vidal and his crew, sir."

"Oh, them. Have we done anything about the skimming?"

"Not yet. It's on the list, sir."

"We assume a little graft in those positions, but he has become too greedy. I don't recall him being a trading type of person, either."

"Gunnery, sir."

"So we need to augment things. Let me think about that. Next topic."

"Yes sir. We have some news about Jake Stewart."

"Yes?"

"He's in jail, sir."

"What for?"

"Starting a fight in a bar."

"He started a fight? Did he win?"

"No. He was beaten up. The bartender fingered him for starting it."

"Any charges for damage?"

"Nope. He got beat up pretty quickly without breaking anything."

"That's a skill of sorts, I suppose."

Jose tapped his comm and paged through some reports.

"The bartender reported to the Militia that he'd been drinking heavily, made a scene, insulted a group of four men, and picked a fight with them. They beat him like a drum, then the bartender got involved and zapped one of them. That one got hurt. He's still in the hospital, but the others got out before the Militia patrol arrived."

"Did the patrol take issue with that?"

"No, they figure the bartender was within his rights and the others had bolted. And Jake was too busy being beaten up, so they aren't charging him."

"If the men weren't around to complain, then what's the charge?"

"Drunk in public. We could bail him out." Jose looked at Dashi and cocked his head.

"Don't. Did Doucette get what we asked for?"

"Good pictures, sir. He and his team followed the two shooters back to their lodging. They can take them out anytime."

"Good. Those are dangerous people. I want them off my station. Tell Doucette to arrange to grab them, and to do it where Colivar can see. That should show him how serious we are. No shooting, though. Jose, how long till they let Jake Stewart go?"

"Two days at the most, a day if they need the space."

"I see," said Dashi. He flexed his steepled fingers again. He spun his chair around to face the viewport. Jose was silent while Dashi pondered.

"Jose, hire that ship."

"Yes sir. And the crew?"

"Keep the regular crew, but fire the contractors that report to Vidal. Then tell Vidal to expect a Militia section shortly."

"Yes sir. We'll have to buy those positions in the Militia."

"Do it."

"Vidal will be unhappy."

"I find I can bear his unhappiness with equanimity," Dashi said. "Call our Militia friend and tell him we are very interested in his new program, 'Militia service in lieu of prosecution.' We're so interested that we want to subsidize the initial training run. Find out what it will cost to put a test section of three people through."

"Yes sir." Jose made more notes on his pad.

"The test section should be ready to go this week."

"Yes sir."

"Keep Jake Stewart in jail."

"Sir? How?"

"Put some pressure on that bartender. Tell him somebody is going to get charged if that man in the hospital dies. Could be him. Could be somebody else. See if he'll change his story."

"Change his story to implicate Jake?"

"Yes. And get me the Militia reports for the last week."

"Yes, sir. Ah, the bar charged three hundred credits for schnapps onto Jake's credit chip. Should we challenge that?"

"Schnapps? Vile stuff. Nope. Pay it and then take it out of Jake's pay."

"He's not fired?"

"Of course not. Keep him on the payroll, just leave him in jail for now."

"Yes sir." Jose went and opened the door but paused before leaving.

"Sir, that bar is well known for fleecing new arrivals, at least to station people."

"Yes, but Jake wasn't a station person, was he? He wouldn't know."

"Did you know what would happen, sir? The fight?"

"I didn't know anything, Jose," Mr. Dashi said. But then he smiled. "But I do remember the day I got my first corporate credit chip, Jose. Good times."

***

Jake came to consciousness slowly. His mouth was dry, and he needed to use the bathroom. He sat up, which was a mistake. His head began to spin and he felt his stomach revolt. He rolled over and fell to the floor with a thud.

His side hurt a lot. So did his stomach. He saw a toilet not far away. He crawled toward it as his stomach spasmed. If he could just get to the bowl. . . .

Nope, he couldn't make it. He tried to roll onto his face so he wouldn't spew on himself, but the pain forced him back onto his side. It felt like his entire stomach erupted through his throat and splashed down his shirt and onto the floor. He heaved again and again, till only a clear fluid dribbled out. Slowly, he managed to pull himself to the toilet for the last few heaves, but then slouched back onto the floor. His stomach felt better, but his ribs and fingers felt worse. And he was having trouble seeing. Very, very carefully he rolled onto his side, trying not to move any of his chest muscles, until his cheek rested against the cold floor. That floor was the best thing Jake had ever felt. So cool, so relaxing. He smiled and drifted off to sleep.

Sometime later—he couldn't tell how long because his comm was gone—a beeping sound woke him up. The built-in comm screen by the door was flashing. He poked at it a bit and got a list. Disturbing the peace. Felony assault. Anti-social behavior. Causing bodily harm. Discharging a weapon.

Jake didn't remember a weapon, but the rest sounded right. He turned toward the mirror. His eyes were black and blue, and his nose looked crooked. The side of his face was covered with dried vomit, as was most of his shirt. His hair was matted with it. He took a deep breath, which was a mistake because his nose was plugged as well, and the smell caused him to gag again. This time he made it over the sink before spewing. He dropped to the ground, grunting as the sharp pain in his hands and his ribs caused him to roll onto his back. He hadn't quire realized where he had puked before, but he knew now, because it formed a pile in the middle of his back.

He lay on his back and stared up at the ceiling.

"How did your first day at work go, Jake?" he said out loud.

***

Jake had crawled onto the bed and lay still. He tried not to move. If it was possible to fail more spectacularly on his first job, he didn't know how. He'd never been that drunk in his life before. He remembered the fight, a bit. He clearly hadn't won. Why had he started a fight? Why had he drunk so much? What was wrong with him? He had an uncle who had been the station drunk. The man had ended up losing his arm in a mining accident. After that he'd spent all his time cleaning the corridors and drinking all the cleaning solution he could steal until he died in his sleep a few years back. Was Jake going to end up like his uncle? He was already in jail. Would they keep him here? He'd be stuck in jail for a long, long time. TGI would fire him, of course. And then what? He'd be on-station with no job. He'd have to become an itinerant crewman, and that hadn't worked out well for him before.

Well, nothing to do but wait and take his medicine.

His comm screen beeped. Jake looked over. Incoming message. He sat up, very slowly, and pressed the button.

It was Jose.

"Hello, Jake."

Jake just nodded. He couldn't talk.

"The charges against you are serious. You hurt one of those men badly. He's still in the hospital."

"Oh."

"TGI is going to have to cover the damage. Did you at least get the info chip?"

Jake tried to speak, but he couldn't. He looked down and shook his head.

"I figured." Jose paused and didn't say anything.

Jake gulped in air and managed to choke out, "I'm sorry."

"That's it? You're sorry?"

Jake just nodded. He couldn't look Jose in the eye.

"Not enough, Jake. Not nearly enough. Mr. Dashi is dropping you from the special program. You're out."

Jake was trying very hard not to cry. He managed a nod.

"There is the matter of the money you owe TGI, as well as the damages and charges against you," Jose said. "Mr. Dashi still feels some responsibility for you. So, rather than leaving you in jail, he's pulled some strings and got you into the new indentured service program the Militia is offering. You're going to stay in the Militia until you work off your jail sentence. They'll pick you up tomorrow to begin your training. Do you understand?"

Jake nodded but didn't speak.

"If you fail the Militia training you are going to go to jail. Mr. Dashi says there is a possibility that you might be sent south. Don't fail the training, Jake."

Jake nodded again.

Jose reached forward to turn off his screen but stopped. "One more thing, Jake."

Jake nodded a third time.

"You have vomit in your hair. You should clean that up." The screen went black.

***

Less than a week later, Jake stood looking at the dazed man on the deck. Zeke wasn't knocked out, only stunned. Sergeant Russell hauled him to his feet, shook him a bit, and gave him some water. Then he started them all running around the gym. Zeke and Suzanne had never been in zero-G before, but they didn't take long to figure out how to move. At first, they slammed into the corners and tripped trying to slow down, but after only a few circuits of the gym they emulated Jake by bouncing off the walls and hopping around the corners and changed from bounding leaps to a sliding shuffle.

Once they reached a level of basic confidence, Sergeant Russell yelled, "Follow me," and headed out of the gym. For the next hour they swarmed around the station, up and down ladders, from high gravity to low, from the core to the rim. Jake didn't feel tired. The sergeant clearly wanted to teach them to move in variable gravity, not to build physical fitness. Eventually, they returned to the gym.

"Line up," bellowed Sergeant Russell. "Right here." He pointed. "All right, you maggots. Listen up. For the next week you're going to learn basic Militia space skills. Low gravity and zero-G movement. Skinsuit training. Basic firefighting. Hand-to-hand combat. Shotgun, revolver, and rifle training. And boarding operations." He paused.

"Sergeant, why are there only three of us?" asked Suzanne.

"Did I say you could ask questions? I did not." Sergeant Russell screamed.

Suzanne was undeterred. "It is a good question, Sergeant. Normally there are more of us. Is this not true?"

The sergeant rounded on Suzanne, took a huge breath, and began to open his mouth. Then he stopped, closed his eyes, and shook his head. "I'm too old for this shit," he muttered. "Yes, that's true," he said in a normal voice. "We do one class a month for fifty people. But you three are some sort of special deal. Only the three of you, and only for a week. Then you report to your ship."

"Oh," said Zeke. "Which ship?"

"No idea," said the sergeant. "Stewart?"

"Yes sir?"

"Don't call me 'sir,' I work for a . . . never mind. 'Sir' is fine. I watched you. Did you grow up on a station?"

"Yes sir."

"Did you work outside, in a suit?"

"All the time, sir."

"Wait, your accent. Are you a Beltie?"

"Belter. Yes sir."

"Beltie, Belter. Whatever. So, no need for movement training. Ever fired any weapons?"

"A shotgun. Once." Jake shivered. He had blown out an airlock window and killed a friend.

"Not enough. We'll cover that. You two, LaFleurs." The sergeant walked to stand in front of Zeke.

"Yes, sergeant."

"You're ground pounders?"

"From the surface, yes."

"Ever fired weapons?"

"We come from the verge, sergeant. We've shot rats."

"Revolvers or shotgun?"

"A little of both."

"Okay, movement for you, then." He paced in a circle for a moment, hands clasped behind his back. "Here's what we'll do. Today I check you out on everything— movement, fighting, weapons, all of it. Any questions?"

"Sergeant?"

"Yes, LaFleur."

"What is a maggot?"

The next few hours went by quickly. Jake clearly outclassed the LaFleurs on anything involving space movement, including, to his own surprise, zero-G fighting.

"Don't get too cocky," said Sergeant Russell. "You just understand gravity better. If you meet somebody with real zero-G experience, they'll eat you for lunch."

The afternoon was not as successful. Shooting at things was clearly not Jake's forte.

"The target is over there, Stewart," yelled Sergeant Russell, pointing.

"I see it, sir."

"If you see it, why can't you hit it?"

"I don't know."

"Look, it's easy." Sergeant Russell took the revolver from him. "Just point the gun, focus on where you want to shoot, and gently squeeze. . . ." BANG. Dust blew up from a dent in the middle of the target. "Try again, Stewart."

Jake raised the gun, squinted, aimed, and pulled the trigger. The weapon jerked up in his hand. Dust spurted on the wall, well above the target.

"Well, at least it was the right wall," Sergeant Russell said.

"Sergeant, why do the bullets explode? Is it because they are training bullets?" asked Suzanne.

"Frangible. They are made out of concrete. They are frangible rounds, not training rounds."

"But why do they explode?"

"Because we want to hurt people, not spaceships. If you fire a solid bullet at somebody and miss, or if it ricochets, it might put a hole in your ship's hull or destroy your navigation computer or puncture an H-line and cause an explosion."

"But how do they hurt people if they are just dust?" asked Zeke.

Sergeant Russell sighed and shook his head. He removed his revolver from its holster, flipped the cylinder out, and dumped all the bullets in his hand. Then he reached into a pocket on his coveralls and pulled out a handful of bullets with green bands. He carefully loaded them into the cylinder and snapped it shut.

It seemed to Jake that he didn't even aim, but instead just extended his hand out about waist height. BANG. BANG. BANG.

Jake felt an excruciating pain in his thigh and his leg collapsed under him. He landed on his hands but was unable to move his leg at all. It seemed paralyzed, and it hurt.

"Merde," said Suzanne as she rolled on the ground, clutching her leg. "That hurts."

Zeke lay on the ground next to Suzanne, also clutching his leg and moaning. Sergeant Russell leaned down toward him and grabbed him by the shoulder.

"That was a quarter charge. Did that hurt enough, or do you want the full one?" he asked. Then he stood up and smiled for the first time. "Some days, this job isn't so bad."

***

The next few days were exhausting. They started every morning with a run around the station, moving from low to high gravity, up and down ladders. Sergeant Russell made the LaFleurs do it a second time while he took Jake to the shooting range.

"You need more low-gravity practice, and Stewart needs more shooting practice," Russell had explained. He worked with Jake for an hour while the LaFleurs completed their second run, then they all shot together. In the afternoon, they donned the skinsuits and went out on the hull of the station. They climbed up and down the spokes, went along the rim, and moved in and out of airlocks, just for practice. They wore buddy lines, and Jake found himself yoked to Zeke for an hour, then Suzanne for an hour. Zeke had a tendency to jump at every opportunity and laugh as he spun and flailed around.

"Zeke, what are you doing?" Jake said over the channel as he hauled him back to the station yet again.

"I don't really know what I'm doing wrong, Jake. I've never done this before."

"You'll get yourself killed."

"No, mon ami. I will not die like this, I am sure."

"You won't?"

"No, I will not die in space. I will die in some sort of stupid drunken stunt. I even know what my last words will be."

"What?"

"'Hey, everybody, watch this,'" Zeke said, then laughed. Jake had to laugh as well.

"Zeke, watch me. You are taking your second foot off the station before your first is locked. Try this very slowly—unlock one foot, slide, lock the magnet, unlock, slide, lock the magnet, unlock the other. . . ." Jake talked him through it as Zeke began copying him. Suzanne flailed around as much as Zeke did at the start, but Jake didn't mind helping her. When she was spinning around at the end of their tether, Jake had the perfect excuse to stare at her. She looked very good in a form-fitting skinsuit.

The LaFleurs' tendency to leap before looking didn't escape the sergeant. He never let the two siblings yoke to each other. "I don't trust the two of you together," he said. "Stewart's had lots of outside experience. Just do what he does, and you'll be fine." Jake was pleased. At least he could do one thing right.

An entire day was spent on firefighting—reading the signs, operating the foamers. Jake's experience became a bit of a problem.

"Stewart!" screamed the sergeant.

"Yes sir?"

"Why didn't you foam that fire? Why did you flush the atmo?"

"Well, as soon as you see a fire, sound the depressurization alarm, count to thirty, then vent the compartment."

"Stewart, we're on a space station with ten thousand people, most of them dirtsiders who don't have suits. If we vent the compartment, we'll kill most of them."

"Oh."

"Is this a Belter thing?"

"Sir?"

"Do you sleep in your skinsuits?"

"Well, in our emergency bubbles, yes, sir."

"Belters," the sergeant said, shaking his head in exasperation. "Look, in the lower stations, first try to put the fire out, and only vent the O if it seems to be growing. It's a last resort."

"Yes sir," said Jake. The sergeant looked at him. Jake looked back, unconvinced. "Sir, people die in fires. A whole station or a whole ship could burn. Fires have to be put out quickly. If you blow out the O, the fire dies, and only the people too stupid to take normal space precautions will be killed, rather than everybody starving to death if the hydroponics get burned up. I still think it's the best course of action," Jake said, then immediately regretted it as the sergeant stared him down.

"Lunchtime," Sergeant Russell said after several minutes and stalked off.

Jake relaxed. That was stupid. He was only making things worse for himself. Zeke patted Jake on the back as they all began walking to the mess hall for lunch.

"Thank you for your help with the zero-G, Jake."

"No problem."

"Jake, I am confused," Zeke said.

"Yes?"

"I don't know much about the Militia, only what I have seen on the videos, but should not our training be longer than two weeks? Should we not do more military things? Uniforms and saluting and things like that?"

"We're in the Delta Militia, not the Imperial Navy. It's more of a police force than anything else. We're civilians, really."

"I thought we were in the Navy?"

"No, we haven't seen a naval ship in this system in over a hundred years."

"That long?"

"Yes. Even before the abandonment Delta was off the main trade routes. We were more like a waystation for ships jumping through the empty quarter. There weren't enough resources for a full colony, just enough to establish some stations for local mining. That's why we're around a moon and not a habitable planet. And that's why we have such a low population and can't build everything we want."

"Is that why we haven't seen any jump ships in so long?"

"I don't know. The Delta Corporation doesn't know either. Technically, they're not a government, just a bunch of companies running things till the empire comes back. But I don't think the empire is coming back."

"Neither do I. But that doesn't matter. We're in the Militia now."

***

Sergeant Russell kept them busy. The LaFleurs continued to work on moving in different gravity and Jake continued to work on his shooting. Most nights he was too exhausted to talk, even though the work wasn't very physical. The necessary concentration was killing him. The sergeant doubled the LaFleurs' runs in the morning, and tripled Jake's shooting time.

Jake's shooting got worse, not better. All three of them shot at the range in the mornings. Sergeant Russell walked behind them and watched.

"Stewart! Stop trying so hard."

Jake looked up from where he was lying. Today they were working with a type of rifle, which sergeant Russell called a carbine. Jake was tired, frustrated, and angry. His shots were nowhere near the target.

"Sir, I just don't have the knack."

"Everybody has the knack. You just need time and patience. Don't force it. Breathe, relax, aim, squeeze." Sergeant Russell was relaxed, almost mellow, anytime they were using weapons.

Jake tried. Breathe, relax, aim, squeeze. BANG. The bullet smushed against the wall. Three feet to the right of the target.

"Stewart, I've never seen anybody as bad as you."

"Sorry, sir."

"Look, you have no problem with the suit stuff, zero-G, firefighting. You're horrible at unarmed combat, but everybody you'll be matched against is worse and you're experienced enough in low gravity, so you actually look pretty good against anybody who isn't."

"Sir."

"But your shooting sucks. Really, really sucks. I can't

sign you off on this. You're a danger to yourself and others. You're more likely to hit one of your boarding mates by accident than anybody else. I can't let you pass."

"That's a problem, sir."

"You only get this special deal of Militia service if you pass the training. If I fail you, you go back to jail. Do you want to go to jail, Stewart?"

"No sir."

"Here's what we're going to do. First, you're going to promise to never, ever, fire a rifle or a carbine at anybody. Not even in practice. You'd probably kill a bystander or even your captain."

"I can do that, sir."

"Second, you will be required to wear a revolver but you can never use it. Never take it out of the holster. You understand me?"

"Wear it but never use it. Got it, sir."

"You have some skill with the shotgun. And by skill, I mean you at least shoot in the general direction of the right target. We're going to use that."

"Yes, sir. Umm, how?"

"I'll teach you how to run the boarding course. You'll go through a ship simulation and shoot at targets. It will be perfect for you."

"How so?"

"The targets are bigger. It's designed for new recruits who have never been in space, so they always mess up their movement. But you move fast and easy, so you should have a better chance. That is okay as long as you get through the course within the time limit."

"And if I don't?"

"What do you think?"

"Back to jail?"

"You may shoot worth shit, but at least you're not completely stupid. What'd you do to land here, anyway, Stewart? You don't seem like the type to get into trouble."

"I hurt somebody in a bar fight. Put them in the

hospital."

"Huh. And they pressed charges."

"The Militia did. Felony assault, assault with a weapon, and disturbing the peace."

"Felony assault? Stewart, you've managed to surprise me. That's a very serious charge. I wouldn't have expected it from you. Not based on what I've seen here in training."

"No sir. I . . . uh . . . I was drinking."

"Hmm. I see. Well, you must have a good friend out there somewhere to land here. A friend of mine got sent south for felony assault a few years back. You're a lucky kid. Don't waste the opportunity you've been given here. Understood?"

"Yes sir!"

"Take that rifle back to the checkout. I'll see you there in a moment." Sergeant Russell watched as Jake packed up and walked back to the armory.

He shook his head stepped behind the LaFleurs and examined their targets.

"Not great, but good enough. At least all of your shots hit somewhere on the target. You two can pack up as well. Pass the rifles into the armory and you are dismissed for the day."

"Sergeant, I still have five shots in my magazine. What should I do?" Suzanne asked.

"Just fire them off at the target, fast as you want. When you are done I'll see you at the desk." He turned and walked away.

Suzanne lay down and carefully adjusted the rifle on her cheek. She fired five shots as fast as she could pull the trigger. Then she reeled the target back in. It was clear that all five had hit the target, because there were five distinct holes in the target paper. All within two inches of the center.

Zeke winked at his sister, then helped her to pack up.

4

The next day, Sergeant Russell brought them together just before they got in the airlock to practice drills in zero-G. He handed each of them a mop.

"Hold on to these and don't let them go. I want them back. If you lose them, I'll take it out of your hide. Everybody, inside!"

Jake looked at his mop as they entered the airlock and cycled through. What were they going to do with these? There was no water in space.

They stepped outside the lock. Unusually, the sergeant didn't insist on tethers. Once outside, he spoke over the radio. "Listen up, you maggots. You're still completely useless screw-ups, but you occasionally show flashes of competence. Today, training will be a little more realistic. Look back there."

He pointed anti-spinward along the station. A Militia cutter was moored to a truss some distance back. It wasn't attached to a hatch but connected with chains to the truss. The near-side airlock was clearly visible.

He said, "You are the boarding crew and those mops are your weapons." He pointed toward the cutter. "There's your target. Board her. Go!"

He stepped back and waited.

"What?" Jake said.

"Clock's running. You three board her. Get there from here. Keep your 'weapons' with you. Clock stops when all three of you enter the dorsal airlock and cycle in."

"Okay," Jake said. He had jumped to ships before. "This is a little dangerous, so Zeke, Suzanne, we'll just edge down the station and look for a line, then we can send it across and. . . ."

Zeke didn't wait.

"Wheeeeaaaahahhahahha," Zeke yelled, taking a giant push and launching himself off the station, spinning out into the void.

"Formmmidabblllle," Suzanne yelled, diving off right behind him.

Jake froze for a second. He'd forgotten that the LaFleurs were still inexperienced in zero-G, and their joint tendency to leap before looking. Or even after looking. He didn't see a guard ship anywhere, none of their tethers were attached, and they only had a very basic thruster jet package on their back. If they missed the ship, they wouldn't stop until they impacted Draconis IV after their orbit decayed.

"Emperor's balls," Jake said out loud. He dropped his mop, demagnetized his boots, and began to run down the outside of the ring, doing a series of forward rolls to pick up speed but staying close to the station. As he spun, he rolled sideways to keep the LaFleurs in sight.

They had leapt off the station with sufficient velocity to reach the cutter, but they had forgotten that they would spin. They hadn't been able to correct for it, so they flipped end over end as they headed toward the cutter.

They had also not accounted for the fact that the station was spinning below them. Rather than impacting on the airlock, they were going to hit somewhere in the region of the engines, perhaps splashing into the drive nozzles.

If they hit at all and didn't just go spinning out into space.

Jake was able to pick up more and more speed as he hopped along the station. Every time his hands came into contact with a grab bar, he flung himself faster along the rim. He continued on until he was actually past the end of the cutter, and then pointed his feet at a grab bar and landed on it feet-first. He felt his entire body compress as he took all the energy of his run into a giant crouch, compressing down as much as possible while keeping his head up. He sighted on the LaFleurs and exploded out of his crouch toward them.

Now he was heading back with the spin of the station but faster. He crossed the distance toward them. They had done a single push off the station, and it was impossible to accelerate with nothing to push against, so their speed was constant. He timed it so that he intercepted them just as they would have slid past the ship at an angle. He opened his arms wide and grabbed both spinning forms in a sort of loose bear hug as he went by. They all collided, but his higher base velocity won the day, pushing them back toward the cutter.

"Turn toward the ship! Get your feet out. Brace with them. Brace!" Jake yelled.

BANG.

The whole shambling mass impacted with the cutter. Jake easily stopped himself on a grab bar, and Suzanne had landed with a foot in front of her. She grunted over the radio as she banged into a crouch, but the magnets on her other boot caught her.

Zeke was not so lucky. He hit shoulder-first and bounced off with a grunt, but he had lost most of his velocity.

"Zeke, give me that mop! Give it to me!" Jake yelled on the channel.

Zeke nodded his head. He had hit hard, but he understood enough to extend the mop. Jake braced himself on the bar and began to pull the mop in hand-over-hand, until Zeke was able to lock onto the ship.

"Okay, we're all here. Is everybody okay?"

"That was excellent." Suzanne giggled.

"It was. But my shoulder hurts," Zeke said.

"Can we do it again?" Suzanne asked.

"Let's just get inside," Jake said. He led the way as they trooped across the outer hull of the cutter to the airlock.

After cycling out of the airlock, Jake had Zeke strip his suit off so he could inspect his shoulder. Zeke was going to have a giant bruise, but it didn't look like anything was broken. Suzanne had hit hard as well. Jake hoped for an opportunity to inspect her shoulders, but she seemed unaffected by all the tumbling.

"Zeke, Suzanne, you both could have been killed. If you had hit wrong, you could have broken an arm or you neck or something," Jake said.

"Yes, papa. Sorry, papa," Suzanne said. Then she looked at Zeke, and they both burst out laughing.

Sergeant Russell came through the airlock. "Most incompetent boarding I have ever seen! I said you had to board, not how to do it, so I guess that counts. Good thing Stewart was there to catch you, though. And Stewart?"

"Yes, sir?"

"You lost your weapon." He handed Jake a broom. "Don't make a habit of that. Take fifteen, then follow me." He stripped his helmet off and stepped over the hatch coaming.

Zeke watched him go, then turned to Jake. "Thank you very much, Jake Stewart. That was very well done. We could have got in a bit of trouble there."

"More than a bit of trouble. That could have been a lot of trouble. If you missed the cutter you would have ended up circling the Dragon for a few thousand years until your obit decayed and you burned up."

"Well, I don't mind a bit of trouble, as long as there

was a bit of fun," Zeke said. He looked thoughtful for a moment. "Actually, a space burial around a planet doesn't sound bad. I think I would like that."

"It would be better than our coffins getting drenched in rabbit pee every day on the Verge," Suzanne said.

"Rabbit pee?" said Jake.

"Yes, the cemetery at Mont Lapin is full of rabbits. They eat the grass and pee on the graves." She shook her hair out, snapped it over her shoulder, and smiled at Jake. He blinked. She looked very alive right then. "But that will not happen to us. We will go some other way. But not soon." She stepped toward Jake, who was sitting next to Zeke. "Not soon—not with Jake to look after us." Suzanne leaned forward and gave Jake a chaste kiss on the forehead. "Thank you for saving us, ma petit chou-fleur," she said.

Jake watched her as she sauntered off, her helmet swinging saucily at her side. Jake turned to Zeke. Zeke winked, then began to pull his suit back on.

"Zeke?"

"Yes?"

"What's a 'chou-fleur'?"

***

By dinner on the fifth day, they were all somewhat more human. The LaFleurs had improved at moving in low gravity, and Jake seemed a little more likely to kill the person he was shooting at, rather than himself—provided that person stood still and Jake was using a shotgun. Their conversation, which had at first been desultory, became somewhat more animated.

"Sergeant Russell, do you have a first name?" asked Zeke.

"Of course I do. Why?"

"I would like to know it. I like to call people I am eating with by their first name. It seems friendly."

"You would like that, huh. I'll tell you what I like. I like to take people who call me by my first name and hammer them over the head with my food tray until they pass out." Sergeant Russell swallowed the last of his red-green-blue tray, licked his spoon clean, and pushed it into what was clearly a cutlery pocket on his skinsuit. Jake had a similar pocket on his suit—all Belters did—but it was unusual for close-orbit folks to have it. He wondered about the sergeant's background.

"Then," said the sergeant, "I like to kick them in the ribs a few times, maybe breaking one, until they learn that whatever they like, I don't like people I don't know using my first name." He stood up, stretched, and looked back. "But I think neither of us will get what we like, LaFleur. You three are dismissed until tomorrow." He stalked away.

"He is tough, that one," said Suzanne.

"Agreed," said Zeke. "But he is a good teacher. He yells a lot, but he knows his stuff. He showed me things with the rifle I never would have thought of, and he is very patient with us in the skinsuit drills."

"He said he just doesn't want to do the paperwork if we are killed," said Suzanne. "But we are done for the day now. I feel more energetic. What should we do? Should we go somewhere?"

Jake perked up. She was a pretty girl, and since the other male at the table was her brother, there was no competition.

"We could go to the bar and get a beer," Jake said.

"Aren't we in jail? Jails don't have bars," Suzanne said.

"Not really," Jake said. "We're on a Militia base. It's its own ring on the bottom of the station. They use it for docking their cutters and training and suchlike. We can't go up to the rest of the station, true, but according to what I read in the training manual we can move around the base itself, as long as we don't go to the restricted areas, and they are pretty clearly marked."

"And there is a bar?" asked Zeke.

"Of sorts."

Suzanne looked thoughtful. "We have never been in space before. You say we are attached to a larger station? Could we get there? Could we escape this training if we wanted?"

Jake shrugged. He was starting to pick up the habit from the two LaFleurs. "We couldn't go through the core. That's guarded. I suppose we could do a jump from this ring to one of the upper rings, but that's very far, and you'd need to time it right. It would be extremely difficult. And we're escorted when we're outside the base. They would notice if we jumped away. And if we got there, we'd just be . . . well, we'd just be on a different part of the station. We'd need a ship to get off. . . ."

"Can we sneak onto a ship?"

"Not usually. There is only one entrance, and it's usually guarded, or you need a code. And if you aren't strapped down, you'll get hurt very badly when the ship starts accelerating. And there are only a limited number of couches."

"We don't know these things," Zeke said.

"You seem very good in zero-G," Suzanne said. "Could you jump to these other rings?"

"Yes," Jake said. "I've done longer before, when I was working at my old station."

"So, why don't you? You could get away. I'll bet you know how to drive a ship."

"Well, I. . . ." Jake stopped. He could jump away, probably. And he did know how to get on ships. And he could pilot it enough to get away. He didn't need to be here. Was it worth it, staying?

Zeke and Suzanne silently watched the emotions play out on his face.

Jake shook his head. "I'm not sure. I could. But I won't. Not yet." He changed the subject. "Let's go to the bar and have a drink."

"We don't have any money," Zeke said.

"No money?"

"None at all. We are criminals, are we not?"

"Oh," said Jake. "Well, I'm not rich but I can afford a pitcher of beer for us."

"Let us go then, and Zeke and I will tell you of our history as criminal masterminds," said Suzanne.

***

Jake led the way. It only took ten minutes to find the inevitable spacer bar that served cheap beer.

"How did you know this was here?" Zeke asked.

"All stations have a bar with just beer for spacers, and usually they're close to the docks. Most ships don't allow alcohol or drugs on board, so spacers drink as long as possible before reporting back on board. A few bars inevitably pop up around docks. I figured it'd be similar for the Militia. Since you can't leave base without a pass, there's bound to be a bar on base," said Jake.

"You said you came from a Belt station. Are all the bars like this? Where are the chairs?" Zeke gestured around—there were no chairs or tables, just a bar along one wall and high ledges on the others.

"Chairs and tables cost money. Nobody is here for the décor. They want beer and lots of it. Plus, there is less to fight with and to break."

"All about money, then?"

"Well, mass, mostly. If you have to boost it to the station, it costs a lot. Anything heavy is expensive. But you guys don't care about that. Tell me about your 'history as criminal masterminds.'"

Zeke laughed, drained his cup, and leaned toward Jake. "It was a farce. Suzanne and I, we come from a small northern Verge settlement, Mont Lapin. We grow potatoes, carrots, onions, things like that. There are some buffalo in the hills, and lots of rabbits."

"What's a rabbit?" Jake asked.

"Small furry animal, about this big." Zeke held his hands twenty centimeters apart. "They have been modified to eat the native grasses, to keep them from overgrowing, and they don't taste too bad if you catch them and cook them. There is a food-processing factory on-site, and lots of picking machines. Not much work, and only at the plant. We were bored, doing piecework, still in mama's apartment."

Jake was trying to figure out how you cooked an animal. He'd only ever eaten different types of food trays, and the occasional apple or pear. Zeke tapped his glass. Jake refilled it.

"I wanted to go out, see the world. Get away, that sort of thing. So did Suzanne. She is the smart one in the family, so she came up with a plan."

"We decided to enlist in the Militia. They turned us down," Suzanne said.

"Turned you down? Why?"

"No education. No technical skills. No space skills. They wanted spacers. I could have joined the corporate police—they take anybody—but then I'd just be beating up people like my friends, just in different crappy towns. That is no life."

"What happened?"

"Well, we have an uncle in town, Landing. A great uncle, actually, but he was smart, went to the university and got a finance degree. He keeps in touch with the family. He set things up. He told us to get arrested," Suzanne said.

"What?" Jake sat up straight. "He told you to get arrested."

Zeke laughed. "Yes. He is my favorite uncle. Nothing major, he said. Just disorderly. So, we started a bar fight."

"Started a bar fight?" Jake asked.

"Yes. Actually, it was Suzanne who started it."

Jake turned to her. "You started a bar fight."

Suzanne smiled. "Yes. We came in with a few friends. I

picked a couple, a young woman and a man, and walked up to them. I slapped the girl and poured beer over her and told her to stop sleeping with my boyfriend. Then I turned to the man and said he was horrible in bed and asked why was he with this slut. Then I threw his beer over another man. The girl went at me, of course, so I dumped her onto a table. Then Zeke came up and pushed the man into his friends, who joined in, and so did our friends. Then it started rolling around the bar. It was great fun." Her eyes danced.

"Who was the girl?" Jake asked.

Suzanne shrugged. "No idea. I did not hit her hard. She should be okay."

"Was she sleeping with your boyfriend?"

"I do not think so. She could have been." Suzanne grinned. "I had many boyfriends."

"The police broke up the fight and sent you to the Militia?" Jake asked.

Suzanne looked a bit guilty. "Well, there was more. There was a birthday group at the other table, and they had candles."

Zeke interrupted. "Suzanne burned the bar down."

"What?" said Jake.

"It was not just me. You helped. But yes, there was a fire. Then a lot of shoving and running. Nobody was hurt, but the bar was damaged."

"Destroyed," said Zeke.

"Damaged," said Suzanne.

"What happened next? How did you get up here?" Jake asked.

"Well, the plan was we would get thirty days in jail, then our uncle would arrange for us to offer to volunteer for the Militia instead. Young people, just learning, not bad kids, need a second chance, all that. We would have no record and we would get trained, get paid, see some of the planet, get an education, get our teeth fixed."

"Your teeth fixed?" Jake asked.

"The whole family has problems with wisdom teeth. By the time we are mid-twenties they impact very painfully. We all end up with either huge dental bills or lots of pain. We tried to time it so we'd be in the Militia long enough to get our teeth pulled," Zeke said.

Suzanne shrugged. "Instead, we got four years for inciting a riot, plus we have to pay restitution, which we don't have. Our uncle pulled a few strings, and TGI bought us out as indentured servants, then loaned us to the Militia. After TGI paid our bill, they own us for four years. Apparently, TGI has to supply people to the Militia at their own expense, so they took us in and gave us to the Militia. So now we are criminals. But if we go to space for four years, it's forgotten. It's not so bad."

Jake shook his head. "I haven't heard of indentured servants before."

"It's a new thing," said Zeke. "But enough about us. Tell us about your station. We have never met somebody from space before."

Jake told them something of Rim-37. Living at the edge of the rings, just getting by. Being poor. Eating the same food trays for weeks at a time. Mining for nickel and iron and aluminum. His scholarship to TGI. Going to the Merchant's Academy. They were particularly interested in how he made his way to Militia training.

"It all sounds very interesting. You had a scholarship to the Merchant's Academy," said Zeke. "You must be very smart." He poured them both another beer.

"I'm smart about some things but pretty dumb about others," said Jake, thinking of all the stupid things that he had done. "But I graduated and here I am."

"Why are you here, at this training?" asked Zeke.

"Like you, I got in trouble in a bar. I owe some money. So, it was the Militia or jail."

Zeke looked at Suzanne and they both laughed.

"What?" Jake said.

"There has to be more to it than that," Zeke said.

"They do not send you here unless you really screwed up. 'Trouble in a bar' is pretty vague. You must have a better story."

"I don't want to talk about it," Jake said.

"You might as well. We are all here together for now. Did you kill somebody?"

"No. They would have sent me to South Continent for that."

"Hurt somebody?"

"Yes."

"Bad?"

"He's still in the hospital, I think."

"Huh. You are lucky they didn't send you south. But there's more, is there not?"

Jake drained his beer and stared at his glass for a moment. He looked at Zeke. "I had graduated from school with a merchant officer's degree. I had a great job working for one of the corps. My boss trusted me with an important job. It was simple. It was easy. And it was my first one. All I had to do was meet a guy in a bar and take a chip from him." Jake reached over and took the pitcher of beer and poured the remainder into his glass. He signaled for a new one.

"Instead, I tried to impress some girls, got drunk, got my money stolen, got in a fight, and got sent to jail. When they fired me and sent me to the Militia, I was sitting with a busted face and vomit in my hair. Now, here I am. If I screw this up, it's back to jail, and then after jail they'll dump me on some out-system transport and I'll end up back at Rim-37 working on the loading dock, which is what I tried to get away from. That is, if they don't drop me off on a beach on the south continent somewhere with seven days' food and a knife."

"Huh," Zeke said, draining his glass. "Drunk, bar fight, jail. Did you at least get the girl?"

"No."

Zeke helped himself to more beer. "Then it was

definitely not worth it."

***

Jake stopped shooting the revolver and carbine completely and concentrated on the shotgun and the boarding course.

"There are two ways to pass," Sergeant Russell said. "Target shooting with all three weapons, getting an 80 percent average score over all three, or running the course with a weapon of your choice and getting an 80 percent score. There is no chance of you getting 80 percent target shooting, Stewart, so you're going to run the course with a shotgun."

The boarding course was a long hallway to a simulated airlock, followed by a simulated breaching, then another hallway, a turn, through two compartments, ending in a simulated engine room. Targets appeared behind doors, around corners, across halls. Some targets had to be shot, while some had to not be shot. Points were deducted for hitting equipment or bystanders.

Jake went through the course at least twenty times. He was a disaster. Twice he got zero points. Once, he got negative points because he somehow shot all the bystanders but none of the targets. That had never happened before, and they had to call in a technician to reset the computer before the next person ran through. Zeke and Suzanne were running on the course behind Jake, and he was grateful they couldn't see his run or his shooting. He was mortified.

"Stewart," said Sergeant Russell, after Jake had scored six points out of a possible hundred, "if I am ever on a boarding and I see you in my group, the first thing I am going to do, for everybody's safety, is shoot you before we board. That will minimize casualties."

"Thank you, sir."

"I just can't see you passing the weapons part tomorrow. I'm sorry, Stewart, but your Militia career ends tomorrow. Enjoy going south."

"Thank you, sir."

"Don't thank me. I've never met a student I couldn't train. You're my first failure. You're great with zero-G—all that time in the Belt, I guess. Hell, you could probably stop close enough to kiss the bad guys, but you can't hit them from more than six inches away." He sighed. "I think I'll go get drunk and start a fight. You do what you want." The sergeant stalked off but turned before he went out of sight. "Oh, and Stewart—you might be thinking that with your zero-G skills you can jump to the next ring and disappear through an airlock into the rest of the station before somebody catches up with you. You might even be able to pull it off. But you're not faster than a gauss needle, and I've scheduled a live fire drill outside tonight."

"Merde. He sounds serious," Suzanne said. "Will they really send you to the south continent, Jake?"

"They might. I really screwed up my first job. And my boss is angry and pretty powerful. He doesn't like failure."

"Huh. Pour encouregez les autres. We have to save him somehow, Zeke," Suzanne said. "We could help him. You and I could attack the guards, and Jake could run through the gate. Or we could set up a diversion. We could start a fire."

"No fires," Zeke said. "That did not work well last time."

"Okay, no fires. But we have to get him to the other side of the station."

"And then what?" Jake asked. "I'll be in a Militia station with no money. I'll just be stuck there. And even if I get onto a ship, chances are it won't have enough life support for me, and I'll freeze in the dark or get tossed out an airlock."

Zeke nodded. "Suzanne, he is correct. We are going about this the wrong way. We do not plan. We just act without thinking. Jake is not like us. He is clever. He is a planner. Jake." Zeke turned toward him. "You must think clever. What is the clever way to solve this problem?"

"Clever way? What do you mean?" Jake said.

"Something smart. Something that only Jake would think of."

"Yes, Jake," Suzanne said. She grabbed him by the arm. "You will come up with something, I'm sure of it."

Jake nodded in spite of himself. He wasn't so sure of it. But he did like her grabbing his arm.

5

Jake stood at the entrance to the boarding course. It was all automated, he just had to put his card in and charge his test shotgun. The shotgun was loaded with compressed air to give the proper recoil, and a laser was used to record hits. In order to pass, he had to get through the exit point within 120 seconds and have a hit score of no less than 80 points.

Jake started to sweat. Would his plan work? Was it allowed? He knew what the rules said, but would he get away with it?

"Only way is to try," Jake said out loud.

It seemed an eternity but finally the light turned green.

Jake flipped through the door, floating down the hall, his shotgun held loosely in one hand as he spun end over end, coming gently to rest next to a door. He stopped himself with the door frame and braced himself. A target appeared not more than two feet away from him. Jake carefully pumped the shotgun, leaned forward until he was less than a foot from the target, and fired.

Even he could hit a target from eight inches away.

He took the recoil and used it to float down the hallway toward the airlock. He landed next to it, turned to the side where a different target had appeared, then shuffled forward to where he could touch the target with his shotgun, and fired again. Another hit.

He continued in this style through the course. Sergeant Russell was right—years of playing on Rim-37 had given him the skill to float across a room and land exactly where he wanted to be. So, he took the sergeant's advice and kissed the targets. Kissed them with a shotgun.

He was not quite halfway through when the first warning beeped on his comm. Half his time was gone. He needed to speed up. He pushed a little harder for the next few targets. He didn't totally stop to fire, just slowed. Still moving well, he rounded the corner into the fake engineering room. Lots of handholds here, so he was able to jump from fake fusion plant to fake altitude jets and touch his shotgun to the targets. So far he hadn't hit any bystanders. His record was good. He floated up and stopped on a control panel. The final engine room target appeared and he shot it. The recoil caused him to gently float toward the door, but he had forgotten how far away the door was. He stretched out his arm and grasped the door just as the twenty-second warning went off.

He still had one more hallway to go down and out before time was up. The hallway was smooth, with nothing to grab to propel himself forward. He launched himself off a desk and into the hallway, hoping he had enough momentum to get to the other end.

His ten-second warning went off. He wasn't going to make it. He reached out with his hands and legs, but he couldn't touch any of the walls or the floor or ceiling to help push him forward faster. When you were floating you couldn't change direction, but you also couldn't accelerate. Dammit. He wasn't going to make it.

Wait. He still had the shotgun. He rolled over in mid-air so he was flying down the hallway back-first, facing the way he came. He bent at the waist and adjusted his body so his center of gravity was exactly behind the butt of the shotgun. The five-second warning rang out and he fired the shotgun as rapidly as he could pump it. Each expulsion of compressed air added to his velocity. He was flying faster and faster down the hallway. The doorway was coming closer and closer. Just before the final alarm rang out, Jake flew over the threshold, still firing as he cleared the doorway. He did a flip, rolled over a surprised examiner who had the good sense to not move, and did a perfect bounce from the back wall to the ceiling to another wall, then stopped on the floor in front of the examiner. He stood up, handed the man the shotgun, and looked at him.

"Well?" Jake asked.

The examiner pointed over Jake's shoulder. He turned and looked at the board. One hundred points out of a possible hundred, 120 seconds. Pass.

***

The next day, Zeke, Suzanne, and Jake were marched down to the locks by the duty sergeant. Since they were technically convicts, they were supposed to be shackled.

"If you all promise to be good, you can just march with me," the duty sergeant said. "But if you cause me any problems, I'll use the shock stick on all of you and slap you in leg irons handcuffed to your arms and see how far you get with that."

Everybody promised to be good, and they headed out. On the way to the lock, they passed a med station with a lineup outside. A sign read "Immunizations Today." Jake read it with interest. He hadn't seen this before. His station had a bad outbreak before he was born, and the station council had insisted everybody get a whole whack of immunizations, but that wasn't common.

They marched on to the airlock. The display board read "Petrel" and showed all green. The sergeant punched the comm board and conducted a muted conversation with somebody on the other end, then stepped back and waited.

The lock swung open and a curly-haired man in ships uniform stepped out. His nameplate read "Vidal." He wore a serviceable skinsuit, with hard collar and cuffs, and sealed station boots. His shoulder showed the rank of third officer. He had thin gloves and a very thin emergency helmet, the plastic bag type, clipped to his belt, along with a small O cylinder. Jake approved. It was a good compromise. He could move with no restrictions, but in the event of an accidental blowout or emergency he could suit up in seconds and move under his own power for an hour or more with no ill effects, even if exposed to a vacuum.

"Thumb here and they're all yours," the sergeant said.

Vidal reached over and thumbed the proffered data pad.

"Thank you for doing business with Militia Staff Support Services. Have a great day," said the sergeant, turning and hustling off.

Vidal watched the sergeant for a moment and then turned back to inspect the three in front of him. He frowned.

"Attention," he said.

Jake roused himself to something of a straight stance. He couldn't quite remember how to do it. They'd had only one short etiquette class at the academy, and he'd mostly forgotten it. And it was hard to do in a suit.

Zeke and Suzanne exchanged looks, then Zeke turned to the man. "Of course you have our attention, sir. How may we help you?"

The officer's eyebrows rose. "What?" he said.

"We are listening, sir," Zeke said.

"Stand at attention."

Zeke looked at Suzanne, who shrugged. He looked to Jake, who continued to stare straight ahead.

"I don't know what you mean, sir," Zeke said. "We never learned that."

"You never learned to stand at attention?"

"No."

"You three are my Militia boarding party?"

"It would appear so, sir."

"How long have you been in the Militia?"

"Does it matter?" Zeke replied.

"Does it matter? Does it matter?" Vidal was nearly shouting now, his neck muscles nearly popping under his frustration.

"I remind you, you have our attention. There is no need to repeat words."

Vidal stuck his head forward and looked angry, then confused. This interview was clearly not going the way he expected.

Jake cleared his throat. "Perhaps you should check your communication from the Militia, sir. That might clarify things."

Vidal spun his head to look at Jake, then took out his comm and began typing. Jake and the LaFleurs stood there. Zeke started to whistle. Vidal glared at him, and Zeke stopped. Vidal looked back to his comm shaking his head and continued reading.

"Indentured Militia personnel," he said. "Great. Which of you is Stewart?"

"Me, sir," Jake said.

"Drunk and disorderly?"

"It was a misunderstanding, sir."

"Uh-huh. Zeke LaFleur."

"That's me," said Zeke.

"Assaulting the Militia. Was that a misunderstanding?"

"Not at all, sir. We did throw a few punches, but it was all a good-natured sort of thing. I had fun."

"I see. You must be Suzanne LaFleur."

"Yes."

"Arson? You destroyed a bar?"

"Damaged, sir."

"Another misunderstanding? Never mind, I don't want

71

to hear it. I asked for a trained Militia boarding party, and I got you three." He looked up at the clock over the display screen. "We drop in less than two hours."

He shook his head and sighed. "Right, no time to fix this. Okay, I'm Third Officer Bassi Vidal. I'm the third watch officer on the Petrel. I need a boarding team and apparently you're it." He stopped and glared at them. "Now, I was hoping for a trained boarding crew, or at least some people with a little experience. Obviously, that's not what I got. But needs must. Follow me."

He walked along the corridor and gestured through a viewport. A ship was visible hanging between two docking trusses.

"There you have her. Type 2 Far Trader. Double the number of drive nozzles, so she can sustain 2G. We lose a bit in fuel tankage, but the extra acceleration is worth it. Top two decks are bridge, sensors, and crew. Then a sealed hold for high-worth cargo, then second crew deck, then container trusses, then engineering at the back."

"What is that attached to the top? Is that a shuttle?" Zeke asked.

"It's not the top, it's the dorsal side. Emperor's balls. Have you never been on a ship before?"

"No sir. We have been on the shuttle that took us up here, but this is our first time in space."

Vidal shook his head. "Better and better. That's a mini cargo tug. Sealed cab, catcher grid in the front, battery-operated thrusters on the back. We don't need a station crane to shift containers to us. We can go out and get them, chain on, and haul them back."

"Is that a fuel barge on the ventral side?" Jake asked, careful to use the correct terms. He sensed this was a test of sorts.

"Yes. But not just fuel. We've got tanks for H, O, and water for consumption or for reaction mass.

"Why do we need that?" Zeke asked.

"Like the tug," Jake replied. He was aware that he was

the suck-up student but couldn't help himself. "It has an electric pump and hoses, so we can shuttle it down to a station or a cracking plant and suck up what we need, and then go back to the ship. We don't need a fueling dock."

"Shut up, Stewart. I'm doing the talking here," Vidal said. "There are also two broomsticks on the bottom for moving personnel and small packages. The Petrel can trade anywhere. We don't need a full station or a docking ring. We can transfer to another ship or from a mining mill without any other facilities. We're totally set up to operate in an austere environment."

He turned to look at his new crew.

"Which means that you three will not be off the ship very much. Which is good for me. One less thing to worry about. Now follow me." He led the way through the boarding tunnel and onto the ship.

"This is the mid deck. Front of the ship is bridge, computers, and sensors, and cabins for the watch crew. There are three officers—captain, navigator, and me. Three ratings as well, including a medic. Captain is also the engineer. Then there is the pressurized cargo hold. It's not large, but it has locking cages for private cargo." They continued walking down a narrow corridor. "This is normally the passenger deck. There are six cabins here. You each get your own. The passengers are locked out from the security deck while we're underway, so you will be too. There's a galley with food trays through there and an access tube to engineering that goes along the dorsal truss that way. We have space for thirty external containers on our truss system. Engineering is at the back. You're also locked out of engineering. Basically, you'll stay locked on the passenger deck unless I need you. We don't have a brig on board but there's not really anywhere to go, so keeping you down here should suffice. Now, I've got work to do, so stay here and don't get into any trouble." Vidal walked off.

Jake, Zeke, and Suzanne looked at one another.

"We are stuck here, then?" Zeke asked.

"Seems like," said Jake.

"This will be no fun," Suzanne said.

"Well," Zeke said, "you will have plenty of time to read those manuals you love so much, Jake. And perhaps you can teach me some of that electronics that you seem to know about."

"I would like that also," Suzanne said.

Jake looked at her. She didn't seem to be attracted to his looks, but perhaps she might be interested in his brains.

***

Alfredo Gianno de Marchello, captain of the GG trader Bountiful Onion, arrived on his bridge. He was a tall man and wore a custom-fitted skinsuit, with his rank tabs and name impressed directly on the material. Even in the void, he expected his crew to identify their captain and treat him accordingly.

Bountiful Onion was enormous for a ship in the Delta rings. It had not one, not two, but three internal cargo holds between its trusses, and its truss system for containers extended hundreds of meters behind him. There were six decks in the front crew section.

The first officer turned around to look at him. "We'll be ready to drop in minutes, sir. Airlocks are going through final closing and inspection now."

"Very well," Captain Marchello said. He keyed a button on his board. "Cargo—has my brandy arrived and been stowed?"

"Yes sir. In the special lockers, as you requested."

"Good, good." He wasn't a huge drinker, but they would be gone for almost six weeks, and he liked a glass of brandy before retiring in the evening.

The first officer waited for a last light on his board to turn green and then reported to the captain. "Ready to drop, sir."

"Good, good, Vasquez. You can take us out."

The first officer nodded, expressionless. The helmsman let out a sigh of relief, then looked around to see if anybody had noticed. The Bountiful Onion was large, luxurious, and had a huge cargo capacity, but nobody had ever called her maneuverable. And the captain owed his position more to family connections than experience. His helm orders could be . . . erratic. Life would be much safer with the first officer giving the commands.

***

The blonde woman at the table munched on an apple as she surveyed the man across from her. He was carefully cutting up a buffalo steak, a specialty of the house. He had thinning gray hair and a face stained with age. He was at least forty years older than her, and dressed in a neat, fussy manner. He looked like somebody's boring grandfather.

Franz's on the Plaza was one of the most expensive restaurants on TGI main, and it was quite common for successful older executives to dine there for a celebratory dinner. Many male executives brought women young enough to be their granddaughters. Some of these women were actual granddaughters, but most were not.

Nadine took another bite of the apple. It was real and fresh, so it must have been boosted recently, at great expense. She looked at the women sitting at the other tables, categorizing the cost of their clothes, hairstyles, and meals. Nadine wanted those clothes. Her mother's advice would have been to use her looks. But her mother had been one of those women once, and it had not ended well. Not for her and not for her daughters.

Nadine had brains, and she intended to use them.

On the other hand, her mother's advice wasn't totally worthless, so she flashed a thousand-watt smile at the man across from her before she spoke.

"The waiter grinned at me when I came in. What did

75

you tell him?" she said.

"I said I was having lunch with my granddaughter, of course."

They both laughed.

"So, platinum," she said.

"Know anything about it?" he asked.

"Yes. Lots. As much as you want. Do you want to hear about it?"

"Not really."

"I didn't think so. You want me to go get you some?"

"Yes. Lots. As much as you can." He smiled as he threw her words back at her.

"Where?"

"I have a list. About thirty places, give or take."

"I can't pull thirty robberies without it being noticed."

"You don't need to steal anything," he said. He took a drink from a glass. "Ahhh. Fresh-squeezed orange juice. Nothing like it. Want some?"

"Yes, please."

"Are you still drinking that fortified basic?"

"You know I am."

"Much better than the regular stuff." He wiped his mouth and looked for a waiter. One appeared, and he gestured for two more glasses of orange juice. There were no order pads on the table. It was much too nice a place for that.

"That glass of orange juice will cost more than the rest of the meal," the old man said.

"You can afford it. So, how am I supposed to get platinum from thirty places without stealing it?"

"You buy it. Trade for it."

"That's a novel approach, Admiral."

"Don't call me that. I'm not an admiral. Not anymore."

"Okay. But you will be again."

The man put down his fork and stared at her. It was not a pleasant stare. "Yes. Soon enough. But don't call me that. Not here."

Nadine nodded her assent. She cut a piece of steak for herself.

"You went to the Merchant's Academy, didn't you?"

"I went to three different academies at various times. I can trade."

"Good. I'll give you a list. Take your ship, go there, buy what you can, steal what you can't. How soon can you leave?"

"The scout ship needs to be refueled and re-provisioned."

"That's happening right now."

"As soon as that is done, then." She cut another piece of the buffalo steak. If she was going where she thought she was going, it would be a while before she got a decent meal again. "Are you sure of your facts?"

"Yes, we have the GG reports."

"GG gave them to you?"

"TGI bought them from a source at GG, and we . . . acquired them from TGI."

Nadine stopped chewing for a moment, looked at him, and decided not to ask.

"So, TGI has the same info as us?"

"No. We have their info, but we have a few people in place that they don't. We know more about the unofficial sources than they do."

"What about opposition?"

"There will be a big GG trader out there. Armed. And there will be a Militia cutter in the area for at least part of the trip. Also armed. And it looks like TGI is sending their own ship or ships to stir things up. They might be armed too, but not with much. It will be a subsidized merchant, only two turrets, and we don't know what's on them yet, but we will shortly."

"How will you know?"

"We have a contact on board. Not a regular employee of ours, but somebody who takes our money from time to time."

"That's great news. Uh, we only have one turret, with a re-purposed mining laser, and we're not exactly space gunners. If we have a real battle, we'll both be wrecked."

"Don't have a real battle then. Figure something else out."

"Okay." Nadine ate some more of her steak. "Anything else I should know?"

"Yes, I saw a familiar name on the report. A name you've put in your reports before. A fellow by the name of Jake Stewart."

"Jakey is there? That's funny."

"How competent is he? Will he be a problem?"

Nadine laughed. "Last time I was with Jake, I framed him for murder, hijacked his job, shot him in the chest, chained him to our galley, and, after all that, I still convinced him to find some smuggled arms for me and help me steal the payment before taking the blame on himself."

"You shot him and he still helped you?"

"I'm that good," Nadine said.

"You remind me of your mother."

"Don't say that. Don't ever say that." Nadine pivoted her steak knife in her hand so that it was in a stabbing position. She didn't gesture or threaten, but the man noticed and stared at her hand for a moment. Nadine looked down and spun the knife back to cutting position. She forced a smile.

"Great. Go on a trading mission, outwit the competitors, fight a space battle or two, steal what I can't buy, avoid getting shot by the Militia, and get back here."

"That's it."

Nadine laughed. "It sounds like fun, actually."

"It's right up your alley," the old man said.

"What's in it for me?"

"How about enough money to afford to drink orange juice every day?"

6

The first day aboard the Petrel was boring. They were locked in the passenger deck and under thrust the whole time, but there was nothing to do. They did have computer access, and Jake could send and receive comm and information requests from company stations in range.

They were all standing in the galley drinking basic. Jake had to show Zeke and Suzanne how to pull cups from the spigot and then explain how they had to drink it every day.

"Basic contains both hydration and calories. It's water fortified with glucose, nutrients, salt, iodine, and other necessary chemicals," Jake said.

"This tastes wretched," Zeke said, nearly spitting his out.

"Yes. Yes, it does," Jake said.

"Well," Zeke said, "it's not quite what we expected, but we are in space!" The two siblings smiled at each other and clinked their cups together.

"Free trades," Jake said, toasting with each of them in turn. He sat down at the table and began to play with his console.

"What are you doing there, Jake?" Suzanne asked.

"I'm just running a navigation plot to track where we

are going. I'm interested in what stations we will be visiting. I'm also looking into the library to see what training modules are available. I like to study things," Jake said. He looked at the two siblings. "Would you like me to show you how to do all this?"

"Yes, very much so," said Suzanne. Zeke nodded. Suzanne sat down next to Jake and touched his shoulder. She pointed at the screen. "Tell me what you are doing there. How do I do that?"

"Well," Jake said. Her hand made him lose focus a bit. And he could smell . . . soap? Perfume? She smelled of citrus. He shook his head and concentrated. "First, we need to know what station we left at, and how its orbit is described. There are six main components—you can look that up here by typing in the name of the station. Next, we have to track our thrust vector. . . ."

Zeke looked at Suzanne over Jake's shoulder. He nodded his head towards her hand. She winked at him and smiled.

For the next two days, the Petrel flew a series of short hops. Jake followed their progress on the computer, but he and the LaFleurs stayed locked on the passenger deck by themselves.

Inbound to their first station, Vidal called them together.

"This station is too crowded, so we don't get a regular berth. We'll be up in the multi-berths with the Free Traders. Time for you to do what we're actually paying you for."

Zeke and Suzanne smiled at each other, and began a whispered conversation.

"But first, Stewart, in my office," Vidal said.

Vidal started to climb up to the next deck and motioned for Jake to follow. Jake followed him up into a corridor and was ushered immediately into a small office.

"Shut the door, Stewart." Jake thumbed the access panel next to the door and it slid shut.

"I see you grew up on a station. You should understand cargo. What happens around cargo. The last boarding section and I were together for three years. We worked well together. We did some business, you understand? We took good care of each other. Do you know what I mean?"

"I think I understand, sir."

" Last week the Militia called them in for overdue re-training. Do you know anything about that?"

"No sir."

"You three were sent by the Department of Internal Planning. Do you send reports to them?"

"I have in the past, sir."

"I see. Bald guy with a lot of wood in his office, no last name. Do you work for him?"

"Yes sir. I mean, I did, sir."

"That's mighty interesting, Mr. Stewart. Did you know that you are a convicted criminal? All three of you?"

"We know that, sir."

"Good. Because I have to report back on your performance to the Militia. And if I determine your performance is unsatisfactory, you will go back to jail. The Militia might even send you south."

"I don't want to go south, sir."

"Good. So here's the thing, Stewart. Those reports you file to baldy better be good. And you better not interfere with any of my business. If you do, I'll rat you out to the Militia, and there is nothing that baldy can do to stop them taking you back and putting you back in jail. Do we understand each other?"

"Yes sir."

Vidal regarded Jake for a moment.

"Or perhaps I can do better. If you screw up enough, I'll send you out to clean up control lines while we're under acceleration, without lifelines."

Jake swallowed. Crew weren't usually on deck during any sort of acceleration. While the ship was maneuvering, it was too easy to drift off or drift into an ion thruster.

"You see, Stewart, they can't refuse me replacements if you're dead. Think you can remember that?"

"Yes sir," Jake said.

"Good." Vidal opened the door and stepped over the open hatch on the deck. "Now, time to do your job."

***

As Jake and Vidal climbed back down to the passenger deck, Zeke and Suzanne turned quickly around to face them.

"Follow me," Vidal ordered, and together the four of them walked down the corridor toward the airlock.

"Sir, what is a multi-berth?" asked Zeke.

Jake thought he could hear Vidal roll his eyes as he continued walking.

"Usually, a ship like this would have its own airlock," Jake explained in a low voice. "That way, they can shut the doors and isolate themselves from the rest of the station. But a multi-berth's got only one airlock for the whole truss section, and just a hatch for us. The Free Traders use it because it's cheaper and it's easier to move cargo ship-to-ship, which they do a lot."

"It also means it's swarming with thieves—I mean, Free Traders—and anything not tied down is going to get lifted. So, we need guards," Vidal finished, glaring at Jake.

Vidal opened the lock to the cargo hold and climbed through. The cargo hold was a series of metal trusses with attachment points. Some were solid lockers with doors and coded locks. Some were grill works. Higher-value cargo and cargo that needed atmosphere were locked in the hold. Vidal gestured Jake through the upper cargo deck. Jake looked around with interest. He'd never been on the crew deck. He was disappointed to find it looked a lot like the passenger deck he and the LaFleurs were constrained to.

"I have to buy some metals on the station, and I'll need

a guard. Ms. LaFleur will come with me to the Port master's. Mr. LaFleur, you'll be at the cargo lock while they work the containers there, and Stewart, you'll be at the personnel lock. Ms. LaFleur, take a revolver," Vidal said, opening a gun case on the wall. "Mr. LaFleur and Stewart, you get the shotguns."

Zeke and Suzanne looked cheerful. Jake swallowed the lump in his throat.

"Yes sir," answered Jake and Zeke.

Vidal walked out of the room as Zeke handed a shotgun to Jake. Jake checked to make sure that the safety was on. He racked it back and forth. Twice.

"Worried about shooting yourself by accident, Jake?" Suzanne said.

"No. Kind of the opposite. One time I really wanted to shoot somebody, but I didn't know the safety was on, so I couldn't make it work. Then she took the shotgun from me, turned the safety off, and shot me in the chest."

"Merde. Were you hurt?" Suzanne asked.

"No. I had a semi-hard suit on. It just dented my breastplate. But it hurt a lot."

"A girl took a shotgun away from you and shot you? I'd like to meet her. What was her name?" Zeke asked.

"Nadine, and I hope I never meet her again. She got me in a lot of trouble."

"Sounds like fun," Zeke said. "But we are ready for trouble, even though it probably will not happen here. But every time I talk to you, Jake, I learn more interesting adventures. And there always seems to be a girl involved. Did you get this girl at least?"

"No such luck," Jake said.

"Well, who knows, perhaps your luck will change this trip," Suzanne said, cocking a hip. "There are other girls. Was she as pretty as me, do you think?"

Jake blushed and stammered out a reply. Jake wondered if she was flirting with him. He didn't have time to find out because Vidal walked back into the room at that moment.

"Time to do your job. Go. Now."

"Yes sir!" they answered. Zeke hustled down the corridor toward the lower hatch and disappeared from Jake's sight.

Jake walked behind Vidal and Suzanne toward the personnel hatch.

Vidal stopped and spun to Jake. "Pay attention, Stewart. Nobody comes on board except me. Think you can do that?"

"Yes sir," Jake replied.

"We'll see. Let's go," Vidal said and set off. Suzanne gave Jake a smile and a wink as she set her gun belt low on her hip and swaggered off. She had a sort of sway that created a nice view from the back. She turned her head in time to catch Jake checking her out. She smiled and stuck her tongue out at him. He watched her the whole way around the corner, then shook his head. "You suck, Stewart. You're going to die alone," he said out loud.

***

Jake stood at the edge of the airlock and looked around the station. He could see why Vidal wanted a guard. There were probably a hundred ships strewn along the truss corridor. The Petrel looked to be the largest. The uniforms varied from dirty civilian clothes to bits of cast-off corporate uniforms to elegant-looking ground suits. There were food carts, computer-controlled loaders, messengers, random cargo loaders, and booths selling everything from alcohol to knives. People swarmed everywhere. It would be impossible to catch somebody once they vanished into this crowd.

Jake's eyes opened wider as he saw a man walk by with a string of small animals trotting behind him. They were small, four-legged, covered with dark fur, and had short, wagging tails. Dogs! They must be dogs! He had never seen a real dog, only in vids. He didn't know how they survived in space. What happened to them in zero-G?

Jake's mind was wandering, and he tried to focus. He couldn't screw up this job. But this station was so strange compared to stations in the Belt. Back there, there were only a few hundred people, and he had known all of them or was related to them. And they never had more than one ship docked at a time. Strangers stood out. Jake looked around. All the strange people made him nervous. He wasn't really sure what he was watching for. What would a thief look like?

"Fried potatoes, mister?"

Jake was shaken from his thoughts and looked down to find a young girl about two-thirds his height, probably fourteen or so, standing just in front of him. She was very thin, dressed in a patched skinsuit and station slippers. Her greasy black hair was tied back in a ponytail, and she had acne on her face. She carried a plastic tray in front of her, half filled with chopped, fried super potatoes, half with plastic squeeze bottles.

"Full size is only a half credit. I've got hot sauce, mustard, and vinegar to go with it." The potatoes looked greasy and cold, like they'd been sitting in the tray for hours. Even if he was hungry, Jake wouldn't have been interested.

"Not for me, thanks," said Jake.

"You sure, sir? It's tasty stuff," she said.

"No thanks."

"I'll take some, please, young lady, with mustard," said a passing dark-haired man, stepping up beside Jake and holding out a coin.

"Thanks, sir." She turned to offer the potatoes to him in a paper bag. She handed it to him and pulled out a big bottle of mustard and shook it a couple of times. It stuck as she squeezed it. She squeezed harder, and it stuck again. She tried a third time.

SPLAT.

"Crap," Jake said, jerking back and looking down at the big mustard stain on his chest.

"Oh, sorry. Sorry, sir," said the girl, hurrying to help him. "I'm so sorry. It will come out. Here," she said, pulling out a dirty rag and thrusting it at him.

"It's okay," said Jake, taking the rag and trying to wipe himself off.

"It will come off, no worry, sir. Here." She pulled out another rag and handed it to Jake. He leaned the shotgun against the wall and began to mop the mustard off his chest. The girl leaned forward and began to help wipe off the rest, rubbing his chest with yet another rag.

"There, sir. See, it's all gone. Sorry, sorry again." She turned and walked away, vanishing into the crowd.

Jake shook his head and inspected his chest. He could only imagine what Vidal would say if he returned to see a giant mustard stain on Jake's chest. Luckily, it appeared the girl had cleaned it up well. She had been very thorough. He frowned as he thought of her insistence in helping, then reached down to his belt pouch.

Yup, it had been carefully opened, and the few coins and credit chip he had kept there were gone. He cursed.

He had been robbed. The whole thing was a setup. The man must have been in on the deal. Crap. He stood up on tiptoes and scanned the crowd. It was no use. They were gone. Besides, he couldn't leave his post. Jake thanked fate that at least Suzanne or Vidal hadn't been around to see him get suckered. He stepped back to his post and turned around to pick up the shotgun he'd left leaning against the wall.

Crap! The shotgun was missing too.

"You useless imperial turd, Stewart!" Vidal said.

"Yes sir," Jake replied.

"Why don't I just drop you off here with the Militia, Stewart? They can take you back and put you in jail."

"I'd rather stay here, sir."

"Do you honestly think I care what you want, Stewart?"

"No sir."

"Good. Because I don't. Remember that." Vidal ran his hands through his hair and shook his head. "You're useless, Stewart. Can't you do anything right?"

"Yes sir."

"What?"

Jake stammered. "I'm not so good with guns, sir. Or . . . or fighting. But I can do other things."

"Astound me, Stewart. What useless thing can you do?"

"I'm . . . really good at accounting, sir," Jake replied, his voice growing quieter as he spoke. "Paperwork. Research. That sort of thing."

Vidal stared back at him. "Well, why don't you get started on the paperwork for losing a shotgun. It's substantial," Vidal said. He stalked off.

"That could have gone better, Jake," Zeke said.

"Yes. It could have."

"It's not so bad, Jake," Suzanne said. "Mr. Vidal did not seem to like us much at the start. It does not matter what we do—I think he is angry we replaced his friends. This is not a big deal. Nobody on the station died. None of us died. It will be okay." She surprised Jake by giving him a quick hug. He smelled that citrus smell again. Zeke slapped his back, then he and Suzanne walked off to the mess.

"None of us have died. Yet," said Jake. He searched for the proper forms on the computer. "Weapons, deadly, loss of."

7

Jake was sitting in the tiny galley the next morning filling out forms when Zeke and Suzanne came in for breakfast.

"Jake, you wake up very early. Do you like your mornings so much?" Zeke asked.

"I have a lot of work to do," Jake said without looking up from the table.

Zeke frowned at the tray selection. "Work? What type of work? And what is a blue-white-orange? Is it fruit?" Zeke said, popping the foil-covered package into the heating slot."

"Algae, super potatoes, and turnip."

"What is a turnip?"

"You'll see. I don't like it."

"Why do we have so many of these strange vegetables here? Why do we not have those fruits that we see on the vids? I would like to try one of those lemons I saw in the movies."

"Delta is too cold for most fruits. Root vegetables and sea algae. Potatoes. Cold-weather food."

"I would also like to try more fruits," Suzanne said. "And Jake, you did not say what you are working on."

"Vidal dug into my records and found out I graduated from the Merchant Academy, so he's got me reconciling all the cargo and fuel paperwork and filling out maintenance forms and loading manifests. It's all part of my punishment for losing the shotgun."

"You can do that?"

"Yes, I can. It's not fun, though. It's even less fun than normal because Vidal won't let me go dockside to check their lists. I have to do everything from here, which takes five times as long."

"Why is he doing that?" Zeke asked.

"Because he's an ass and he hates me," Jake said. "He's pretty angry. He was really angry about me losing that shotgun. But I suppose paperwork is better than the alternative he threatened me with."

"How did he threaten you?"

"He said he'd leave me on the deck of the ship while we were maneuvering without a line. That's as good as throwing somebody out an airlock."

"That is not good," Zeke said.

"I think things are not going well for him," Suzanne said. "You probably did not notice, but we did not bring anything back. He was not able to buy those metals that he wanted. We came back with the empty hands."

"He didn't? No, I didn't notice. How come?"

"I could not hear well, but he seems to get angry very quickly. There was some dispute about the price, so we just left. He was very upset."

"He didn't offer a higher price? Or try to negotiate more? Maybe offer a trade?"

"No, we came directly back to the ship."

"That's not the way it's usually done. You appear to storm out, but then you come back."

"That is not what we did. I do not think he has done this before," Suzanne said. "But you should be happy, Jake. He was angry even before he learned you lost the shotgun. He was not just angry with you."

"Hmm. I guess so. We should be careful not to antagonize him," Jake said. "He has a lot of power over us."

Zeke smiled at Jake and clasped him on the shoulder. "Too late for you, my friend."

***

Jake had gone back to his cabin to finish the paperwork. A series of angry emails kept coming from Vidal as he trudged through the papers. Apparently, Jake was not only stupid but useless and irresponsible and didn't understand anything. Oh, and he was a poor speller.

Zeke and Suzanne went with Vidal onto the next station. Jake stayed behind doing paperwork and was still there when they came back. He moved out to the galley again, just to be somewhere different. There was a standard gym set of folding bars and small weights at the end of the hallway. Jake had hardly been in the galley five minutes when Suzanne came out and started to stretch before her workout. The stretching was very involved and required a lot of twisting and bending over. Jake found it very hard to concentrate on his work. He wondered if she'd waited until he was out there to start her workout, and why she had to bend over and touch her toes so often.

"Jake, will you boost me up for my pull-ups?" Suzanne said.

"What?"

"Grab my legs and lift me up so I can reach the pull-up bar."

Jake walked over and Suzanne showed him how to lift her up so she could reach the bar. This required grasping his arms around her thighs and sticking his nose ten centimeters from her butt cheeks. She made him stay there until she had completed her set.

"Thank you, Jake. You are very kind." She blew him a

kiss as she sauntered away. Jake was almost certain that she never used to sway that much. He heard a snort and turned his head. Zeke was watching him from down the corridor.

"Sorry, Zeke." Jake blushed.

"Sorry about what, Jake?"

"She's your sister."

"And a very good sister she is. But she is a grown woman, and I don't get involved in those things. Besides, I like you."

"You do? Thanks."

"You would make a good brother-in-law."

"I would?" Jake perked up. Did Zeke know something he didn't?

"Yes. In about ten years. In the meantime, I don't think things will work out the way you want."

"You don't?"

"With Suzanne, things never work out the way the men want. But don't give up hope, you could be the first." Zeke stretched his arms a bit. "You have been very helpful to us, and we appreciate it. You are a good friend, Jake Stewart."

"Thanks, Zeke. I need a few friends right now."

"Why is that?"

"Vidal hates me. I'm a screwup in his eyes, and he's not totally wrong."

"Well, losing that shotgun could have happened to anybody."

Jake looked at Zeke for a moment. "No. No, it could not have happened to anybody. It happened to me because I'm a dumbass."

Zeke sighed. "Okay, I am your friend, but that did seem kind of sloppy. But you are good at other things."

"Hmmph. Paperwork, maybe. But I want to be good at things like you guys are—shooting or burning down a bar or whatever. Every time I get an opportunity, I screw it up. I get beat up or I lose something expensive or I get sent to jail or I end up making my boss hate me."

"Well, at least it was only a shotgun. It is not like you shot anybody."

"I guess so."

"There is still hope for you, Jake," Zeke said.

Zeke looked around for a moment. Jake wasn't sure why, because there was only the three of them locked on this small deck.

"Vidal is very unhappy. He did not bring back any metal again."

"No?"

"None at all. They sold it to somebody else. He left in a rage."

Jake shook his head. "They didn't."

"They did not what?"

"Sell it to somebody else. That's a ploy. They say that they sold it to somebody else to drive the price up."

"Oh. I guess that makes sense. What happens then?"

"You are supposed to tell them to go buy it back from whoever they bought it from, and that you'll pay the difference. It's a standard tactic."

"I did not know that."

"I guess Vidal doesn't either."

***

They were on final approach for the next station when Vidal came down to their deck.

"Listen up. Zeke, you are on lock guard. We've got more things to pick up, and we took on board a sensor computer at the last station for a TGI ship here at Refinery-77. They're expensive and hard to get, so I need two people with me. Stewart, you and Suzanne are going to suit up in your semis and escort me over there. I'll have a revolver and so will you, Stewart. Suzanne, you get a shock stick. I want a non-lethal option in case we meet some troublemakers who aren't worth shooting."

"Thank you, sir!" Suzanne said. "I've never used a

shock stick before. Can I try it out on Jake?"

Vidal laughed over the comm. "Sure, go ahead. Just make sure he's recovered by the time we get started."

Suzanne stuck her tongue out at Jake and grinned.

"Stewart, don't lose this gun as well."

"No sir. I won't," Jake said.

"Excuse me, sir, but why do we have to get suited up in a semi? We'll be inside the station. Can't we just use a regular skinsuit?" Suzanne asked.

"Semis are kind of like armor. Shock sticks won't work on the panels, and it's harder to punch you or hit you with a stick or something. Mostly because it's regulations, to be honest," Jake said.

"Stewart, shut your trap and come with me for your gun."

He followed Vidal up to the arms locker. Vidal opened it up with a thumbprint, and took a revolver, ammunition pouch, and holster out. "Take one and load it up." He turned and began loading his own gun.

Jake took a revolver and puzzled over the bullet selections. There were green bands on some—those were training rounds, so he shouldn't take those. He racked his memory. He needed black bands. He grabbed them, flipped out the cylinder, and loaded six rounds. Vidal came back and, as per regulations, did a visual scan to make sure Jake had not taken one of the two shotguns or the two other revolvers there. "All set, Stewart?"

"Yes sir."

"Get the LaFleurs and meet me at the airlock in fifteen, suited up."

***

Jake, Suzanne, and Vidal marched through the station. Vidal led, with Jake right behind him and Suzanne bringing up the rear. The sensor computer was in a black bag slung over her shoulder. Vidal stopped and linked his comm into the station's net. It displayed a green path to the other TGI ship.

"Huh. Says we have to walk all the way around the outside of this cylinder, a twenty-minute walk. Some maintenance on the shafts. Let's get started," Vidal said, and they began to troop around the circumference of the station.

Refinery stations were big. Giant mirrors concentrated the sun's rays on piles of ore and heated them to boiling, driving off impurities. Different metals boiled at different temperatures, so changing the aspect of the mirrors allowed different temperatures and boiled off different metals. It was the same chemical process as distilling alcohol. Ships tended to want to stay away from liquid metals that might coat their sensors or giant mirrors that would burn them to a crisp, so there was a great deal of distance between docking ports on a refinery. A twenty-minute walk around the perimeter of a station was not at all unusual.

The group marched past a single station crewman walking opposite them. His skinsuit looked like it had seen hard use, and it was patched all over. He slowed, looked at them, then continued walking.

Jake felt a bit uneasy. His hand reached down to clasp his holster, just to reassure himself it was still there. He'd had difficulties in the past on other stations with people who slowed and looked at him, and this part of the station was deserted. He turned around and looked over his shoulder. The crewman had stopped and was watching them.

"That's far enough," said a voice in front of them. Jake turned back around to see a brown-haired man with a tattered skinsuit stepping out from behind a metal truss. His face was dirty, as was the shock stick he carried in his hand. A pinched-faced woman stepped out behind him. She aimed a shotgun at them.

"Give it up," the man said, pointing at Suzanne's bag.

Jake felt his heart race. An ambush. He froze.

"Easy, everybody. Easy, easy," said Vidal as he held up his open hands. "Look, we don't want any trouble, but you don't want to do this. This is a sensor computer, not something you can easily turn into cash. It only fits certain corporate ships, and no corporate buyer will buy it from you if you try to sell it. They'll just turn you in."

Jake couldn't seem to move at all. He knew he should do something, but what? He could feel his breath rattling down his throat. His eyes focused on the shotgun. He could see the hole at the end of the barrel clearly.

Vidal's voice seemed to come from very far away. "We just want to deliver this and get back to our ship. We'll chalk this down to a misunderstanding. You folks were expecting gold or something, but it's just specialized electronics. Useless to you."

Draw your gun, Jake. He had to draw his gun and shoot. That was the only option. Jake began to pick at his holster. It wouldn't open. Why not? It had a snap. Damn it, he had forgotten it had a snap. Stop being stupid and focus, Jake. He banged his chin button to magnetize his boots and grasped the handle of the revolver.

He heard Vidal say, "Suzanne, show them what's in the bag." Jake couldn't see him, though, even though he was right behind Vidal. All he could see was the shotgun.

Suzanne had stepped to the side and begun to unzip the bag when Jake got a firm grasp on his revolver. He pulled it up, crouching in the two-handed stance Sergeant Russell had shown him all those weeks ago. The pinched-faced woman had lowered the shotgun while they talked. Jake faced her, covered one hand with another as he had been taught, and took careful aim at her center of mass. She saw him point the gun at her. Her face turned white as she realized she couldn't get her shotgun up in time.

The sergeant would be proud of him. Staring down the barrel at her chest, he began slowly squeezing the trigger. The pistol jumped up. He brought it back down. He aimed and squeezed again. The pistol jumped back up. Down, aim, squeeze. He couldn't hear the shots at all. Was the pistol even working? Were the shots silent? The woman still hadn't fallen. Aim. Squeeze. Shit, Vidal was falling. He was down. Who had hit him? The shotgun hadn't fired. Aim. Squeeze. Aim. Squeeze. Still up. Aim. Click.

Click?

Jake pulled the trigger. Another click. Again, click. He shook the gun. Empty. The pinched-faced woman looked at her arms, her chest, down, up, then back at Jake.

Jake stood completely still. His hearing came back with a rush as he heard people yelling and a banging noise. Why wasn't she down?

He realized he had just missed a stationary target from three meters away with all six shots.

The woman brought the shotgun up and pointed it at him. Jake felt something slam into his side, knocking him down. The shotgun blast roared over his head as Suzanne's tackle knocked him down. Jake rolled over onto his back, stunned. Suzanne reached for the gun still in Vidal's holster. She pulled it out and faced forward. The pinched-faced woman had broken her gun open and was fumbling for a new shell.

Suzanne aimed Vidal's gun two-handed and fired. The bullet pinged off the woman's arm in a puff of dust, and she screamed and dropped the shotgun. Suzanne fired again and the hit the woman hard on her chest, knocking her backwards. The woman and man turned and ran. Suzanne turned around and aimed the gun just as Jake saw the third man behind retreating. She shot, but the bullet pinged right in the middle of the closed hatch the man had leaped through. Suzanne rolled her back to the wall and looked back to the front, but that man and woman had vanished.

Jake shook his head. His hands and wrists hurt from the recoil, and he was a little banged up from hitting the floor. He leaned toward Vidal and saw blood pumping out from his arm. He pulled a spray can of wound-seal out of the emergency pack on his belt and pointed it at the wound. He sprayed it carefully over where the blood was pumping out, and it immediately made a sterile plastic seal. The blood ceased pumping. "It's okay. It's not bad. We'll set you up," Jake said.

At that moment, the decompression alarm began to ring. Jake didn't feel his ears pop, so it couldn't be a big drop, but they needed to get out of there. Suzanne jumped up to collect the dropped shotgun and grab the comm computer.

"Don't worry, we'll get you out of here," Jake said, trying to pull Vidal up to his feet.

"Stewart," Vidal said.

"You'll be fine. It'll hurt when we move, but we need to get behind an airlock."

Jake frowned as a thought struck him. "Did the other guy have a gun? I didn't see one. The shotgun missed."

"Stewart, what type of ammunition did you load?" Vidal said. His tone was pinched and strained. He must have been in a lot of pain.

"Ammunition? What do you mean, sir?"

"He means," Suzanne said, coming over and helping Jake pull Vidal toward an airlock, "that you loaded solid shots, not ship ammo. And you, or your ricochets, punched a hole in a wall or bulkhead or whatever they are called, and that is why the alarm is ringing."

"I don't understand. Did the other guy shoot him?"

"No, Jake," Suzanne said. "You fired solid shots and they bounced off that truss. You shot him."

8

Jake sat at the desk in his quarters, miserable. Vidal had been treated at the clinic on the station. They had doped him up, removed the bullet, screwed his bones together with titanium plates, stapled his skin and muscle together, sprayed it with sealant, and sent him back to the ship. His arm was in a foam cast, but it should heal. The other TGI ship had sent a crew to collect their new sensor computer. After spending an unfruitful hour looking at mugshots, station security had let Jake and Suzanne go.

There was a knock on his door and then Suzanne came in before Jake could even say 'go away.' She was humming to herself as she walked over and sat on Jake's bed.

"That was so exciting, yes? So much fun." Suzanne was downright beaming.

"It was?"

"Yes, the talking, the shooting, the yelling. It made my blood race."

"You weren't scared?" asked Jake.

"No, I had no time to be scared."

"I had plenty of time to be scared. Well, thanks for saving me. If you hadn't tackled me, that shotgun would have hit me full-blast."

"It was nothing. You would have done the same for me. In fact, you did the same thing, of course. That is why you shot at that woman."

"I shot her because I was so scared I wasn't thinking right. No, you did the right thing, Suzanne. You saved me and Vidal. I'm the one who shot the man who can make my life hell, and nearly killed everyone on that station."

"That is true." Suzanne preened a bit. "But even though you made a mistake, you tried your best. Your hands were shaking, but you were so close that if you had had the correct bullets you would have hit that woman."

"My hands were shaking?"

"Yes, you were shaking."

Jake replayed the scene in his mind. He'd thought he was cool and focused, in control. Of course, if that had been the case, his clothes wouldn't have been drenched in sweat by the time he got back to the ship.

"You didn't feel afraid at all?"

"No, I was excited, but in an alive way. I could see everything clearly and in focus. Things seemed to slow down."

"Things seemed to stop completely for me," said Jake. "I was very nervous. Scared, even."

"It was a dangerous situation. This is why I wanted to join the Militia. Get away from home, go to exciting places, have adventures."

Suzanne stood up and did a quick foot shuffle, stretched her shoulders back, and took a deep breath. Her smile beamed around the room.

"But Jake," Suzanne said, pulling Jake from his thoughts, "why did you load with solid-shot bullets rather than ship bullets?

"Good question. Station security asked me that too. I guess I forgot which colors meant what. I thought the black bands were frangible."

"No, that is the green bands."

"Aren't green bands the training rounds?"

"No, that's blue. Don't you remember Sergeant Russell's talk?"

"I guess not. I screwed up. Again. Vidal is sure to want to throw me out an airlock now."

"Well, yes. That is possible." She smiled and walked over to his door, humming again.

***

"Stewart, what do you have to say for yourself?" Vidal asked. He sat behind his desk as Jake tried not to sweat all over the floor. Vidal still looked a bit pale, and he kept playing with the hard foam bandage on his arm. Jake noticed that he had a holster with a revolver on, and that it was unsnapped.

"Nothing, sir," Jake said.

"Screw up once, shame on you. Screw up twice, shame on me. Screw up three times, who do I blame? My parents? The schools? Sunspots?"

"Just me, sir."

"Do you know how much paperwork I'll have to go through to get this sorted out, Stewart?"

"No sir."

"It will go on for months."

"Yes sir."

"Do you hate me, Stewart?"

"Me? No sir. Why would you say that?"

"Well, you cause me great administrative distress, and, oh, you shot me. Tell me why I shouldn't just throw you out the airlock right now!? I could claim you threw yourself out because you're so stupid! No one would argue with me. After all, how idiotic do you have to be to mix up solid shots with ship bullets!"

Jake said nothing. What could he say?

Vidal put his head in his hands for a moment.

"What I want to do, Stewart, is to dump you out an airlock. I want that so badly. But for some crazy reason, I've decided not to. So, I'm sending you back to jail."

Jake didn't say anything, but he felt his stomach drop.

"Did you hear me, Stewart? You're going back to the Militia."

"Yes sir."

"Go back to your cabin. You'll stay locked down there

until I can find a station with a Militia crew to take you back to jail and leave you there to rot."

***

Jake sat on his bed and stared at the ceiling. Another of his monumental screw-ups, that was for sure. He began to take stock of his life thus far. He'd done well in school, but any sort of activity outside of studying or doing low-level cargo work had been a dismal failure How had he managed to screw up everything in his life like this?

"Because you suck, Stewart," Jake said out loud. He dug under his bed. He thought he had three beers stashed away from a case Zeke had smuggled on board from an earlier station. Three beers should get him drunk, almost.

Jake popped open a beer and began to type out an analysis of what had gone wrong in his life. Other than "You're an idiot" and "You can't hold your liquor" and "Every time you try to impress a girl it goes horribly wrong," he wasn't making much progress. He was self-aware enough to realize that blaming all of his problems on booze and women didn't make him unique. He had a list of other minor issues like "You have poor hearing," "You have poor fashion sense," and on and on. But these didn't seem to be enough to explain his current predicament.

He finished his first beer, popped open another, and began two new lists. One was "Things I can do well." The other, "Things I screw up all the time." The first list was mostly administrative, trading, and computer activities. The second list was much longer. He sighed and finished off the second beer, his head starting to get that warm, fuzzy feeling of a good buzz.

Perhaps he should just give up booze? A lot of his problems involved booze. Of course, by that logic he should give up women as well. Mind you, that seemed to be happening for him whether he wanted it or not. And to be honest, most of his mistakes happened even when he was stone-cold sober.

Jake opened the last beer and thought about his future. Years from now, after he got out of jail—if he ever did—maybe he could get work as a deckhand on a long-haul ore carrier. As a criminal, he wouldn't be able to get any sort of licensed job, so he'd only be able to get the lowest-paying deckhand gigs. He'd spend his life attaching and detaching containers, his biggest joy in life being his bi-monthly shower on a station, until he was finally killed in the inevitable industrial accident.

What a wonderful life. Huh. He looked at his last beer. It was barely touched. Okay. Enough self-pity, he thought. He poured the third beer down the sink, drank a big glass of water, and started a new list titled "What I need to do to get out of this mess." He began to type.

***

Bang, bang, bang. Jake woke up and yawned. Somebody was at the door. Suzanne and Zeke were standing there, holding a pile of food trays. Jake recognized a red-green-blue and some of the non-cooking ones.

"Jake," Zeke greeted him. "Here, we thought you could use some food. Vidal told us he is sending you back to jail. How are you doing?"

"Not well," Jake said.

"Yes, we can see that," Zeke answered, picking up the discarded beer cans on the table.

"I'm going back to jail as soon as Vidal can manage it. He's turning me over to the Militia. Which is actually good, because if it was up to him I think he'd dump me out an airlock."

"Yes, I am also surprised Vidal did not throw you out," Zeke said, giving Jake a long look and smiling.

"What is that look for?" Jake said. Zeke shrugged and

looked over at his sister.

"Vidal will not shoot you," Suzanne answered, as she looked around for somewhere to put his trays, finally just dumping them on his bunk. "Why should he do that?"

"He hates me. Oh, and I shot him."

"Well, yes, shooting him did make him angry. But you did fix him up after. And killing you would be a lot of paperwork, which he hates almost more than you. At least, that's how I explained it to him."

"You? Explained. . . ?" Jake stumbled. He rubbed his head again.

"How are you keeping busy, my friend?" Zeke asked.

"I was . . . making a . . . a list of things I'm good at doing. That's what I've come up with."

Zeke looked at his list. "Researching cargo paperwork. That is it?"

"Yes, that's it. And shooting people by accident."

"Jake, that is silly," Suzanne said.

"Oh, I forgot to add 'get drunk and start a fight in a bar.' Sorry, that should have been 'lose a fight in a bar.'"

"You are not the first man to ever do that."

"Or the first woman, either," Zeke said, smiling at his sister. Suzanne smacked his shoulder.

"Jake, things are not so bad. What about all those repair things that you know, how to fix things on spaceships, the electronics and mechanical things. And you can pilot small ships, and navigate, and you know all these trading and administrative things. You just made a mistake, that was all. Bassi is being hard on you, but he is just frustrated at not being able to buy these metals he needs. I have been trying to help him, but I don't the things you know, Jake."

Jake stared at Suzanne. "You have been trying to help him?"

"A little."

"You call him Bassi now?"

"Bien sur."

Jake shivered for a second, then changed the subject. "How long till we get to TGI main?" he asked.

"TGI main? Why?" Zeke said.

"There's a big Militia base there. Closest one. He'll dump me with them when we arrive."

Zeke shook his head. "I don't think that we're going there. Vidal said we were going out orbit, if I heard him right. Suzanne and I will be busy for the next few days. He has more cargo to pick up. We have different stations to visit."

"Going out orbit? That's curious."

A beep sounded from Suzanne's comm.

"Jake, we have to go." She leaned forward and gave Jake a big hug. She felt good, warm and soft, and he smelled the citrus again. She pulled away and gave him a smack on the arm. "Do not worry so much, Jake. You are clever. I'm sure you'll think of a solution, just like with the course in training." She smiled and shuffled out the door with Zeke. Jake heard them lock the door to the passenger deck as they left. He was all alone.

Jake thought about that as he munched through the hot tray. He logged into the system and began to take stock. He was locked out of the comm sections, but he was able to follow their course on his computer. They were going out system, moving from station to station.

With nothing else to do and with Zeke and Suzanne busy with Vidal, Jake spent his time working on his lists. He had to admit, Suzanne was right about some things— he was good with the computers.

He read the general mass reports out of boredom, and began to crosscheck reports. When a ship disposed of garbage it was weighed before disposal so that changes could be noted. Same when cargo was loaded or unloaded. The Petrel wasn't taking on any supplies at these stations, and just minimal trash was removed. Jake looked for changes in cargo mass. There weren't any. In fact, cargo showed no changes at all. Almost like they weren't picking up any cargo. After they had been travelling for two days, they still hadn't altered course anywhere near a Militia base. That was an interesting development. Jake kept digging into the reports and thinking about what Suzanne had said before she left. 'Think of something clever.'

***

Jose finished signing for the packages the courier had brought up. Unlike anyone else he had ever worked for, Mr. Dashi received actual packages from the surface and from other orbital stations. The packages were special. They required a code to open, and entering the wrong code more than twice set off a small explosive, obliterating what was inside but not your hand.

Probably.

"Sir, your packages have arrived," Jose said over the comm.

"Bring them in, please," Dashi said.

Jose stepped through the heavy door and closed it behind him. It snicked closed. Jose had learned that this meant that electronic signals couldn't leave the room.

"Sir, I have some news on Jake Stewart. I put it in your regular report, but I would like to discuss it with you."

"Of course, Jose. What has happened to Jake?"

"He shot Mr. Vidal, by accident."

"I see."

"Vidal has him locked in quarters. But from the tone of the report, I think Vidal would rather toss Jake out an airlock."

"I see," Dashi said and smiled. Jose was an expert on Mr. Dashi's smiles. This was his teaching smile, and it meant 'go on.' Jose continued.

"It appears Jake shot him by accident, but Vidal thinks it was deliberate."

"Why would he think that?"

"Perhaps he thinks you sent Jake to kill him."

Mr. Dashi pushed his chair back and rolled his shoulders, then clasped his hands together.

"Why would I do that?"

"I think Vidal doesn't just work for us. I think he is passing information to the other corps."

"Go on."

"Vidal is paranoid. He must have something to hide. . . . Wait, that's why you sent Jake there."

"Do you see Jake as an assassin?"

"No sir. I don't think anyone who has met Jake would see him as an assassin. You would have to be extremely paranoid to think of Jake as an assassin. Of course," Jose nodded. "Brilliant. Jake is so obviously not an assassin that sending him there would not upset an honest man. Only somebody with lots to hide would worry about a guy like Jake."

"Yes. Very good, Jose. Perhaps someday you will have my job."

"I don't think so, sir. I think you will be here for a long time."

"Things don't always work out as you plan, Jose. Ask Jake."

"Yes sir."

"How is Vidal doing on collecting those metals?"

"Not well, sir."

"We need those metals. I don't care what happens to Vidal, but we need those metals. Send a request for an update. Remind Vidal of what his quotas are and ask how close he is. Query his answers. Be aggressive. Send him another list of stations you have located in the outer Belt. Shake him up."

"Yes sir. Uh, we'll have to skip one of the stations on my list."

"Why?"

"They've put themselves in quarantine, sir. Some sort of outbreak. But they didn't have much to start with."

"Very well."

"And Jake, sir?"

"What about Jake?"

"Should we tell Vidal to let Jake go?"

Mr. Dashi smiled. "No, Jose. Jake is exactly where I want him to be, for now."

☐

9

"Tell me more about what Vidal is trying to buy at these stations," Jake said. They were sitting together at the mess table in the middle of the passenger deck. Jake had been stuck down there for nearly a week. He had hardly seen Zeke and Suzanne. Vidal had been keeping them busy, so Jake had been alone nearly the whole time. But that had given him time to do some research and start to come up with a plan.

"Metals," Suzanne said, shaking her head slightly. "We go out with Vidal and sometimes others in the crew. These are very small stations. I have never seen anything like them. A couple of dozen, never more than fifty people. Very small."

"Yes, but what is Vidal buying? What kind of metals?" asked Jake.

"Well, nothing so far. Vidal meets with people on these stations and tells them that he wants to buy a bunch of refined metals, names I don't know. Iridium, maybe. Some others that start with R?"

"Ruthenium? Rhodium?" asked Jake.

"That sounds right. What are they for?"

"They're used in superconductors and some specialized magnets for fusion plants. Most corps have a machine to refurbish existing magnets to keep their fusion plants running. They plate them with a special plating, and rhodium and ruthenium are part of it."

"Oh. Is that why they are expensive? Is that why Bassi is having such a hard time? He is getting grumpier and grumpier these past days. I cannon cheer him up," Suzanne replied.

Jake felt some heat rise to his cheeks. He didn't want to think about how Suzanne cheered up Vidal. He shook the thought from his head. "Well, they didn't used to be expensive. Not cheap, but not much more than, say, gold."

"He is offering two or three times the price of gold in TGI credits for them. He has got very little so far."

"TGI credits? He's trying to use TGI credits on GG stations?" Jake smiled.

"Yes, is that a problem?" Suzanne said.

"Well. . . ." Jake tried to stifle a small laugh behind his smile. "Where are they going to spend it?"

"Spend it? Anywhere," Zeke said, finally looking up from his tray and joining the conversation.

"Nobody out here will take TGI credits. Not without a huge discount."

"A discount? Why?" Suzanne asked.

"Didn't you discount other corps' credits on the Verge?"

"Well, on the Verge we took TGI or GG or CT credits. But we never discounted them," Zeke said.

"That's because you could verify them."

"Verify them?" Suzanne asked.

"Money is money. How do you verify it?" Zeke said.

Jake looked at him for a moment. Were they serious? Money is money? How naive could somebody be? Then again, they were groundsiders and always had network access. He started to explain.

"Zeke, on Delta money is issued by the corporations.

Each corporation creates a special electronic form that says . . . well, basically it says 'this is money.' They issue a form that says it's one hundred credits, and they sign it with their secret password. There are two passwords—a public password and a private password. They publish their public password, so anybody who wants to check it just makes sure they can decode it with their public password. That way you know the money is real."

"That makes sense," Zeke said.

"Wait, you said this is an electronic form. Can't people copy it? People can make hundreds—thousands of copies of these forms," Suzanne said.

"Right, they could," Jake said. "But what happens then is when they give it to me, they want it to go only to me. I have my own passwords too. That's what you have when you have your own payment chip—that's just a chip with two passwords as well. They encrypt it with my public password and send it to me. Then I'm the only one who can spend it. When I spend it and give it to you, I use your public password to further encrypt it, so only you can use it."

"But how does that make it secure?" Zeke asked.

"Well, when you receive the money, your chip backtracks the purchase—it uses the public passwords to track back the source of the money, all the way to the beginning. We all have to sign it."

"Sounds complicated," Zeke said.

"Wait, but how do I know you are really you? These passwords are secret, correct? Can't you just make up passwords and steal the money?" Suzanne said.

"They're not actually called passwords. They're called certificates. And I do make them up, but then I register them with one of the corps—GG, or TGI, or OWA, or whoever. That way, you're guaranteed that it's somebody the corps do business with."

Suzanne and Zeke were quiet for a moment. Zeke looked confused. Suzanne was thinking.

"So. . . ." she started. "So . . . if I have one of these certificates from GG, it's no problem to take GG money, because I can prove it's real. But if I don't have one from TGI, there is a risk that it is fake."

"Exactly," Jake said. "Not a great risk, because you can validate some of it or you can pause the transaction until you're in communication distance to check a certificate or just tell the person that you take the money pending approval. But you charge a premium for the distance."

"How much is the premium?" Suzanne asked.

"It varies. At my old station, if it was a good customer and you're just waiting for a comm window, you might charge 5 percent for the trouble. If it's a new customer or supplier but a reputable company, you might charge 10 or 15. If you don't know the person at all and it's a certificate issued by a minor corp, you might discount 50 percent or more. One of the guys in the finance department made a living discounting chips 90 or 95 percent."

"What do you mean?" Suzanne asked.

"If you gave him a hundred-credit chip from somewhere strange, he'd give you five credits and take a chance that it was valid. He didn't risk that much, and when he won, he won big."

"We didn't do anything like this on the Verge," said Zeke.

"Yes, but you were on a planet. You could always authorize the certificates. And if you wanted to spend the credits, you could just take the monorail into Landing and trade them there for things."

"Yes, so?" Zeke said.

"Mostly only GG ships come this way. Where will they spend TGI credits? GG won't pay them face value. They'll discount them. These folks will lose money on every trade if they have TGI credits, and they know it."

"Oh," Zeke and Suzanne said in unison. Jake wasn't sure they actually understood everything he'd said, but that didn't matter.

"Is Vidal offering to trade instead of giving TGI credits?"

"No. We aren't offering to trade anything," Suzanne said.

"Wowzers," said Jake.

Suzanne cocked her head at Jake. "What are you thinking, Jake?"

"Suzanne. . . ," Jake began and stopped. He couldn't believe he was about to ask this. "You've become . . . close with Vidal, right?"

Suzanne smiled. "Yes. Bassi has been very unhappy and his arm continues to pain him."

"Bassi? You're on a first-name basis now?"

"Yes, why not?" Suzanne arched her eyebrows. "That's what I call him off duty when we—"

"That's fine," Jake said. "Not my business. But—"

"Are you jealous, Jake?" Suzanne smiled.

"Jealous?" Jake said. "Why would I be . . . never mind. Look, Suzanne, when will you see Bas . . . I mean, Vidal next? Outside of work, I mean."

"We have dinner together many nights. We are to meet later tonight."

"Yes . . . okay . . . great." Jake shook his head. Suzanne continued to stare at Jake and smile.

"Don't take it too hard, Jake," Zeke said. "She likes it if you are jealous. It is what she does."

"I'm not. . . . Suzanne?" Jake asked, ignoring Zeke's comment. "Does he have a list of places to go and buy things from?"

"He does. I heard him talk about it."

"He said something about not being able to go to some of the places because of the orbital geometry," Zeke said. He looked proud that he had used the word "geometry."

"Can you get me that list?" Jake said, looking at Suzanne.

***

"Let me understand this," Suzanne said.

Jake was standing in his room staring at the list of stations Suzanne had brought back that morning.

"You want me to ask Bassi at dinner tonight to provide you with all these supplies because you have a plan to get all the metals he needs, if he agrees to not send you back to jail?"

"And not to shoot me or throw me out an airlock or any other means of untimely death, yes," Jake said.

"And the supplies that you are asking for will be used to trade for metals."

"Yes."

"And this will work. Why is that?"

"Because I'm a Belter," Jake said, straightening his back. "I know how these stations work. I know how they buy and what they buy. I know what they need and what they just want. And I know how much they pay."

"How do you know that there will be enough of the metals Vidal needs at these places?" Zeke said from his spot on Jake's bed, tossing an empty cup of basic up to the ceiling before catching it again.

"We're a far trader. We have more range. We can go farther and self-lead at these remote sites. There are not a lot of ships that can do that, so we'll be able to go where there isn't much competition."

"That makes sense. But he will ask why you are doing this. What you want. He does not trust you."

"I want out of jail, for good. I want a good recommendation from Vidal. If this works, he can recommend dismissing the charges against me, and you guys, too. We'd be free."

"He can do that?" Suzanne asked.

"Yes. If he says we did our work satisfactorily and that we've fulfilled our debt, then the charges are dismissed."

"You are sure?"

"Yes. I looked it up."

"Of course you did," Suzanne said, smiling, in that way that made Jake's knees wobble just a little.

"It clearly states in sub-section—"

"We trust you, Jake," Zeke said, standing up and draping his arm over Jake's shoulders. "Now we must wait and see if Vidal likes my sister's smiles as much as you do," he said, smacking Jake on the back and walking out of the room, his sister grinning as she followed him.

***

Vidal stared at Jake from across the desk.

"I hate you, Stewart. You know that?"

"Yes. Yes, I do, sir." Jake nodded.

"I'd like to see you sent south."

"Yes, I know that." Another nod.

"And I'd like to shoot you myself."

Jake didn't nod at that. He didn't want to encourage that line of thinking. Mostly because he figured Vidal probably could get away with it.

"I know that too."

"But instead of that, you think I should listen to this plan you have, is that right?"

"Yes sir."

Vidal stared at Jake silently for a moment, then looked at his screen. "Our mutual friend, the bald guy, has sent out a message. He gave me some more stations to try. And he sent a directive," Vidal said. "This ship is to come back with as many platinum group metals as we can get our hands on."

"Yes sir. If I understand things correctly, specifically ruthenium and rhodium?"

"Yes. Money is apparently of no object, but that doesn't seem to matter to these lowlife stations."

"Yes sir. I grew up on stations a lot like these. I understand what they're looking for."

"Well, then. By all means, Stewart, enlighten me," Vidal

said. His eyes bored into Jake's. Jake began to sweat but kept his focus.

"First of all, offering them TGI credits won't work. They can't use them out here. And if they do, they have to discount them too much."

"I figured that part out myself, Stewart," said Vidal. He sighed. For the first time he actually looked weak, defeated. "If they don't want credits, what do they want, Stewart?"

"These stations all receive visits from corporate ships coming out here with standard packages of supplies. They can trade bulk, low-value items for needed things like food and such. And they do it in corporate credits they can use for other things. We're not doing that, so we have to sweeten the deal."

"How so? I gave them 20 percent off standard prices. That's a great deal."

"Will you get into trouble if you sell all the goods at a loss, sir?"

"A loss? Well, no, not really. From what I understand, our bald friend wouldn't care if we sold most of the ship, as long as we got the rhodium and other metals he wants."

"Okay, sir, so here's my plan."

Jake explained. First, they had to have something to sell. He wanted to break all the food containers up into person-year packages. Rather than having them all one type of tray, they'd split it into half red-green-blue, the cheapest, a quarter red-green-white, the next cheapest, and so on, down to 5 percent of the coveted buffalo-meat trays. Then they'd combine those with miscellaneous items from the other cargo containers and trade the whole thing as a package.

"Ten pairs of pants? Ten shirts? Two skinsuits? Two kilograms of wood? Ibuprofen? That's a package?" Vidal asked.

"Yes sir. They don't need a full container with five hundred shirts. That would last them forever. It's just a waste of storage space. If we sell them ten person-years of food, they can always eat that. Belters like to carve wood because it's hard to find. They have a problem making clothes, and they can always use an extra skinsuit. They'll probably re-trade that to some other Free Trader or wandering miner. And consumables like medicine are always welcome."

"I see. And you want this delivered in a container-sized unit?

"That's the way it's done in the Belt, sir. We swap containers. Ours for one of theirs."

"And what about this pricing?"

"It will make sense to them, sir."

"I don't necessarily agree, but for the sake of argument, let's say that I do. How do we get out there?"

Jake wanted the supplies delivered via a TGI freight ship to a rendezvous in empty space. There, they would unload all the attached containers in free space and then begin re-attaching them. This allowed him to put the containers full of fuel and O in specific places on the truss systems so that fueling hoses from the barge could reach them directly. With everything positioned correctly, the Petrel could self-fuel herself without moving anything. Then he wanted to dump the empty containers onto the other ship and arrange to partially unload two external containers into the internal storage before the other ship arrived. He had scanned the cargo manifests of where they were going and had an inkling of what would be needed, so he wanted to load some items that otherwise would have gone away.

Vidal listened quietly while Jake talked, then asked, "Where did you learn to shift cargo like that, Stewart?"

"In the Belt, sir. But I also was on a tramp, a Free Trader, for a time." He had actually been running from a warrant for murder and had taken a crew slot on a tramp trader under an assumed name. His crew boss took advantage of his illegal employment to steal half his wages, and Jake had been nearly killed by a container that broke loose and almost crushed him.

"That's not in your records."

"No sir. It isn't," Jake said.

Vidal waited for Jake to say more, but Jake kept his mouth shut. Vidal shook his head. "Okay, Stewart. I don't like you, but this is the best plan we've got. But remember this." He paused. "If this doesn't work, well, accidents happen every day."

10

They met the TGI freighter in orbit. In the beginning, Vidal handled the coordination of the whole event, but by the end of their thirty-hour window Jake was organizing everything and Vidal was just overseeing.

Suzanne and Zeke had great fun leaping around with the regular crew and helping them attach and detach containers. Jake was more stressed than he'd ever been and didn't sleep for the entire thirty hours until they got underway. This was his last chance. If his plan didn't work, Vidal would ensure Jake never made it out of jail, if he even made it to jail in the first place.

The next station they arrived at was what Jake would call a family station—about thirty people, probably all related to each other. Family stations usually started from a couple and their kids working a particularly rich claim. These family groups had usually split off from larger stations they were in some sort of orbital resonance with and would meet up with in orbit two or three times a year to swap needed items. They were usually of two types— families that were working a rich ore body with cash to spare and general happiness, or families where the best days were over and everybody was broke, bitter, and violent. All happy families are alike, but every unhappy family was different.

Since there were only thirty people on this station, it didn't have a docking truss. Jake, Zeke, and Vidal met in the airlock. Vidal glared at Jake and made an "I'm watching you" gesture with his fingers, but he wasn't overtly antagonistic.

"We need to take the broomsticks," Vidal announced.

"Yes sir," Jake said. He'd been driving broomsticks since he was five.

"What's that?" Zeke asked.

"Two-person transports," Jake said. "A cargo box, control panel, seats, and a simple reaction system. Battery-operated powerplant charged by the ship."

"I've never ridden one," Zeke said.

"We have some time before we need to go down. Stewart, you take one, and Zeke can take the other. Show me what you've got."

"Yes sir," Jake said. They edged around the hull to where the broomsticks were charging and disconnected them from the ship. Jake hopped on and waited until Vidal gestured at him, then used the jets to gently lift the broomstick above the ship, spin around in a 360-degree roll, and then float gently to Vidal's side.

"Not bad, Stewart. Zeke, you're next," Vidal said. "Let's see how you do."

Zeke was able to disconnect the broomstick and climb on board, but everything else went wrong. He began spinning in a circle but took way too long to find out how to counteract the spin. Then he set off forward and began a rolling motion as he headed away from the ship.

"Follow him, Stewart," Vidal ordered.

Jake followed behind as Zeke headed toward the station. He was spinning from side to side and having difficulty correcting. He over-corrected and began a slow spin in the other direction. Jake caught up with him.

"Small pulses, Zeke. Small pulses."

"I am trying," Zeke said. He pushed the throttle again and the broomstick accelerated toward the station.

"Zeke, slow down," Jake said.

"Where are the brakes?"

"There aren't any. Spin around, then fire the thrusters."

Zeke complied but didn't quite correct the way he needed to. His broomstick bumped into the door, nozzle first. It tipped to the side, and Zeke slowly floated away. Jake came up and nudged Zeke's cargo basket. Gently working the controls, he managed to stop the spin and brought them to a halt relative to the station, then pushed them toward locking bars nearby.

"Good thing you are around to help me out, Jake," Zeke said.

"He has to be good for something," Vidal said as he came up behind the other two.

The airlock equalized, and they walked inside.

"Greetings, traders," boomed the man in front of them. He was tall. Very tall. They were all tall, in fact, and all black-haired. Perhaps a dozen people filled the foyer behind the airlock, men and women ranging in age from about twelve to . . . old—perhaps sixty or seventy? They all wore green skinsuits. Neat but patched.

"I'm Carl. I'm the purser here at Cavernon Station."

"Third Officer Vidal. This is Stewart and LaFleur."

"Those aren't GG colors you're wearing."

"No, they're not."

"I see." Carl paused and waited, but Vidal didn't elaborate. "What can we do for you folks?"

"Mr. Stewart here is a trader assigned to us. He has some items that you might be interested in."

"Oh?" Carl sounded skeptical. "We can talk, certainly. But we don't need much. GG keeps us well supplied. Maybe a few trinkets. But I notice you and Mr. LaFleur here have what looks like revolvers on your belts."

"We do." Vidal nodded. "And they'll stay on the belts

unless there's some sort of problem. But I don't want any problems, because I'll bet there's a revolver or two on your side as well."

Carl smiled. "Of course there is. We're honest people but not stupid. And there might be a rifle trained on you from somewhere as well. Are you okay with that?"

"We are. I think we understand each other."

"Good. What have you got?"

"Mr. Stewart speaks for us. Jake?"

Jake stepped up to the fore and began chatting with Carl. He listed the items in his standard container load. The food, clothes, wood, a few items of furniture, some solvents and cleaning chemicals they had stolen from engineering, a painting. Carl had a reasonable poker face but some of his family didn't. Jake caught a few whiffs of interest. He ran through the list twice, once listing all the items available, then a second time, giving more details of each of the items. Carl was a veteran negotiator, not expressing interest in anything but querying to cut down their value.

"Food is in factory containers?" Carl asked.

"Sealed boxes of fifty," Jake said.

"Standard is one hundred. What's the size range of those clothes?"

"Two extra-large, three large, three medium, two small."

"We run big here. Small is not too useful for us."

"You have children," said Jake. "They are small. And you can trade them to your buddies."

Carl smiled and nodded. "You're young, but you've done this before."

Jake finished up. Carl waited, too experienced to name a figure to start with.

"All of this can be yours for one hundred thousand credits."

Carl frowned. That figure was high. Very high.

"I thought you'd done free trading before, Mr. Stewart.

You know that's not even a moderately reasonable starting bid."

Jake shrugged. "Maybe not. But that's the charge if you want to pay credits."

Carl recognized an opening when he heard one. "What if we trade?"

"What have you got to trade?" Jake asked.

"Son, we're obviously a mining station. We have nickel, copper, tungsten, iron, aluminum, a little gold and silver, other metals. What say we offer you. . . ." Carl went on to name a package of metals, mostly nickel, at inflated prices. Jake waited, ignoring the amounts and values. He had something else in mind.

"What do you say to that?" Carl asked.

"You have a few things we're looking for," Jake said. "Here's our counter. We'll trade gold at one thousand credits a kilogram." That was a decent price for gold but not great. "But we'll trade two thousand credits a kilogram for platinum or palladium." That was double the going rate. "Three thousand a kilogram for iridium, and five thousand for ruthenium or rhodium. In trade goods." That was almost ten times the going rate.

Carl blinked at that. "Well, we normally sell our rhodium at twenty thousand a kilogram."

The game was on.

They came to an agreement quickly. Carl wanted to buy things from these fools before they came to their senses. He wanted a second, identical package. Jake was willing but said they had only allocated one for this station, and they bickered back and forth. Finally, Jake agreed to 7,500 credits per kilogram for rhodium and ruthenium, provided they paid for everything in those metals. Carl sent the family scurrying, and they sweated back and forth for forty minutes, but finally he had to confess. "Mr. Stewart, that's a fair offer but we can't fill it all. We'll be about 900 grams short, even including our partially refined ore."

"And that's assuming that we take your assay values on

the partials as correct," Jake said, "and we had agreed to set that aside while we talked. I think it's too high, but we'd have to do a full assay to prove it. How about this— if I take all the metals offered, including your partials, you'll still be short about 6,350 credits or so, plus whatever I think I'm owed for the assay. I'll take the metal plus ten thousand credits, and I'll take GG credits."

"All the metal and eight thousand GG credits," Carl countered.

Jake had known those assay values were overvalued.

"Done, if you'll give us half the cash in mixed small GG coins and notes, and half in electronic certificates."

"Agreed," Carl said, extending his hand.

"Agreed," said Jake, shaking it. "Who's coming up with me to inspect the container?"

"My assistant, Terry," said Carl. "Mr. Vidal, your boy here strikes a hard bargain, but he's fair to deal with. Will you and Mr. LaFleur be our guests for dinner?"

"Ah, thank you very much, but we ate on the ship and we have to get moving."

There was a general stirring of the crowd and a number of frowns. Jake interceded. "Excuse me, Carl, I have to chat with my boss for a second." He grabbed Vidal by the arm and steered him back toward the airlock.

"You have to stay," Jake whispered. "You're a hostage. When one of their people comes up to the ship, we leave one of ours down here to make sure that we don't leave with a family member or hold them for ransom. You'll go with him to eat and also count the money. The money stays with you down here until their guy confirms that the container has what we say it does and he watches as we push it off to them. They'll probably send him up with a broomstick and a couple of chains and they'll tow up a replacement container, but they won't release you until the container they bought is broke free of us."

"Oh. I didn't know," Vidal said.

"It's the standard way things are done. Nothing

unusual. But they won't proceed with things unless you stay down here and count the money."

"How do I determine that we have the right type of ore?"

"Can you read a spectroscope?"

"No, but I bet you can." Vidal turned. "A little scheduling issue, Carl, sorry. Jake and I will be staying for dinner with you." The crowd relaxed. "Your fellow Terry will go up to our ship with Mr. LaFleur." Vidal looked at Zeke. "It might be best if Terry drove."

***

Everything had gone as planned, and the Petrel pulled away as soon as the replacement container was secured. Carl and company had already secured their container down-port, and everybody gave big, cheery farewells over the radio.

"Stewart, maybe you've finally found something you don't completely suck at," Vidal said, though Jake could hear the begrudging strain behind his words.

"Yes sir."

"Stewart, why did you ask for the credits?"

"They'll have lots of GG credits on account that they can't use, and we can use the loose change—I have an idea at the next larger station we go to that might let us pick up something."

Suzanne and Zeke had been listening. "That was very smart, Jake. I wish we could do that. You are very good at trading." Suzanne gave him a hundred-watt smile. Jake blushed a bit.

"Um, well, I'm good at this. I wish I was better at the shooting and stuff. That's more important."

"Yes, it is," said Vidal, rubbing his healing shoulder.

"Yes sir," Jake said as Vidal stalked away.

"Don't believe him, Jake," Suzanne whispered. "Lots of people can shoot guns, but without you doing this we'd be in big trouble. You got more out of this one station than we got out of six. Bassi is just jealous."

"Trading is easy. Anybody can do it if they try."

"Not me," Zeke said. "I have no idea how you managed all that. You shouldn't downplay your skills, Jake."

"It's nothing," said Jake, looking at the floor.

Zeke and Suzanne looked at each other, shrugged, and changed the subject.

**

Captain Marchello marched around the ship for his weekly inspection. He enjoyed the opportunity to don his best uniform, and he insisted that all the crew do likewise. He had a full-time valet to shine his boots and iron his tunic and ensure that all the appropriate decorations were attached. His crew did not, but this fact did not stop him from issuing demerits and criticism for any uniform infractions he found.

His days were full. Every morning he awoke and was served a breakfast cooked by his personal cook (officially rated as a third gunner) and perused reports from the last few shifts. His first officer attended him during breakfast but was not invited to eat. Bacon was expensive, and the captain had none to waste. The first officer wrote down the captain's criticisms and directives, incorporating them in the "order of the day" that the captain issued after breakfast. All officers were required to acknowledge receipt and understanding. Then he examined personal comm traffic when in range. It vexed him that they were rarely in range of any high-speed comms, and soon they would be totally out of reach. He had business interests to follow.

After that, he had the officers' gym cleared and exercised. Then a shower—with no water limit, of course—and a massage from his own personal masseuse.

(Like the cook, valet, aide, and a few others on the captain's personal staff, the masseuse was listed as a member of the gunnery department. The chief gunner despaired because only he could actually aim, fire, or repair the ship's weapons, but the captain was unmoved. When would he need to shoot at somebody?)

In the afternoon he played chess with the doctor or the first officer for several hours. They both lost—the doctor because he didn't care for the game at all, and the first officer because it was the politic thing to do. In the evening he listened to classical music while dining on whatever his chef had prepared and then read with his evening glass of brandy until retiring. The watch officers knew better than to call the captain after dinner—all calls went automatically to the first officer. The traditional weekly meal with his officers had been suspended after the captain referred to the food served to him as a form of moose feces and spat it out. Since that was better food than the officers regularly ate, the first officer had arranged to schedule mandatory drills or maneuvers during every normal invitation night since. He told the captain that the officers would be delighted to host him again but the necessities of the ship precluded it.

The captain and first officer marched through the main cargo hold where a number of containers of high-value items had been stored. He smiled with content as he examined the piles of copper and tungsten ingots. His family owned 17.5 percent of the profit from these lucrative far trading voyages. In fact, his personal presence was the result of a complicated arrangement that allowed each allied family to supervise one voyage every few years. He was paid a premium over his regular salary to do so.

Captain Marchello may have been a bit of a dilettante regarding ship handling, and his grasp of items affecting crew moral was poor, but he understood wealth when he saw it, or didn't see it.

"First, what is going on here? Why are these cages not

full?"

"As I'm sure the captain knows, we have been paid mostly in bulk metals this trip—tungsten, titanium, nickel, iron, and aluminum. It's all in my reports, as I'm sure you read, sir."

The captain never read those reports. "Yes, I know that, of course, but why no precious metals?"

"We have some, sir. A little gold, some silver, but the others, particularly the platinum group, seem to be in short supply. But it doesn't matter, sir. We are still meeting revenue goals. One ton of iron is the same value to us as 50 grams of gold—more value, really. We have plenty of space and we get an excellent price on the iron, better than the gold. These people know they can use the gold anywhere, but we're the only market for the bulk shipments."

"Yes, but the portability issue?"

"We have plenty of room, sir. We're emptying our holds selling our goods at an excellent mark-up."

"Yes, but. . . ." The captain paused. How did he explain that he had planned to raid the precious metals bin and carry off a briefcase worth of it, paying for it at the same rate they paid the outer stations at, then selling it at the vastly inflated inner system value? This sort of embezzlement was winked at as long as it was kept to a reasonable amount, say, what he could fit in a suitcase. A few kilograms at most. But on a few kilograms of iron he might make a mere fifty credits. A few kilograms of platinum, however, he'd rake in fifty thousand. He needed those bins full so he could steal—he meant, buy—some of it.

"It is unusual. Why would the numbers be down? What do you make of it, First?"

"I'm not sure, sir, but I can inquire at the next station."

"Do so."

***

Nadine punched the altitude jets and cursed as the ship rocked. It had taken two tries to mate with the airlock.

"You okay?" asked Jen. Jen was the other person on the bridge. The two of them were pilot, navigator, engineer, and gunner if necessary.

"Yes, just tired."

"You and me both. We can't keep up this up with just the two of us."

"We'll keep up. We have to."

"Too true," said Jen. "I can barely imagine us getting what we are promised."

"I have an excellent imagination. I have no problem imagining it," said Nadine. Her thoughts turned to orange juice. "Where do oranges come from?"

"What?" Jen asked. "Old Earth, I think."

"But how do we get them on Delta?"

"They don't grow on Delta. It's too cold. They're made in those, what do you call them, greenhouses, where they heat the air to keep it warm all the time. They're really expensive. It costs a fortune to heat those places, and they need special radiation shielding and special lights, something to do with the spectrum. Why do you ask?"

"Never mind. Let's get the show together. Meet you at the airlock."

She suited up in five minutes and they collected together in front of their side of the lock. They were met by a hulking man in a reinforced hard suit carrying a shotgun. He looked like a medieval knight from the old vids. His name tag read "Demitrios."

Nadine tilted her head up and gave him her best smile.

"Ready?"

"Yes, boss."

"Good. What did I tell you?"

"Stand still and look scary. Don't talk. Don't attack anybody unless you say. Don't kill anybody. Hit them before I shoot them."

"Good, what else did I say?"

"That if I mess up you'll kill me in my sleep."

"Good, good. We understand each other."

Jen was carrying a metal attaché case. It had reinforced hinges and clasps and a thumbprint lock, and it was connected to a harness on her body by a short chain. The same harness had two revolvers in quick-draw holsters. She hefted the case up. "All set. Ready to do my thing."

"Showtime, people." Nadine stepped into the lock, and her crew followed her. Nadine didn't carry any weapons.

At least, not any visible ones.

She carefully closed and locked the ship behind her, then spun the inner wheel. It opened wide into the station to show a tall man with black hair. Two equally tall men with shotguns stood behind him.

"I'm Nadine. We spoke on the comm."

"I'm Carl."

"We're in a bit of a hurry, so we'd like to move right along here."

"Fine with me. We'd like to inspect the goods."

Jen applied her thumb to the lock on the case. There was an audible click as it opened and she flipped it forward for Carl's inspection.

Carl leaned forward and reached into the case. Inside were six revolvers anchored by clips. He unclipped one and removed it, opened the cylinder and spun it a few times, then closed the cylinder, cocked the hammer, and dry-fired it. The action worked easily, and the hammer dropped with an audible click.

Nadine cleared her throat. "Six revolvers, five hundred rounds of ammunition, four hundred frangible, one hundred solid shot."

Carl nodded. "As discussed."

Nadine smiled. "Now, Carl, as regards payment, we have some definite preferences."

11

The next few stations went as smoothly as the first, and Jake got to demonstrate why they needed the GG credits. They had just finished trading at one of the larger stations. More formal, it had a truss, its own refinery mirror, and a station office. Their discussion in the office went well and their usual overpayment for platinum group metals—PGMs—went through, but Jake had been reviewing a number of the reports before arriving. He spoke to Vidal on the way out.

"They should have more."

"More what?" Vidal asked.

"More PGMs. You sent me the, uh, reports you were given, and there were some production reports and assay reports. Given what they're refining here, there should be more. More metals."

"They said that was all they had."

"Yes, well, I think it's a ploy. Suzanne?"

"Yes, Jake?" Suzanne said. Either Zeke or Suzanne accompanied Jake and Vidal on these buying trips. Jake could probably have done it by himself, but Vidal still had a few issues with Jake being alone.

"Ask Zeke to go to the cargo office and collect all the GG credits in the office. They're in one of the lockers."

"You just leave the credits laying around, Stewart?" Vidal asked.

"We have a ship stuffed with platinum bars. Who's going to steal company house credits?"

Vidal didn't say anything, which Jake was learning to take as approval.

They arrived at the airlock, and Zeke took the bag of PGMs from Vidal. At this more sophisticated station, they seemed much more relaxed about the transfer.

"They must be more trusting," Suzanne had said.

"Or they have a high-powered laser sighted on our bridge and ready to fire at any time," said Jake.

"Or that."

Jake swapped his bag for the GG credits and handed some to Suzanne, Zeke, and Vidal.

"What's your plan, Stewart?" Vidal asked.

"Just follow my lead," Jake said and stepped back out of the airlock.

The station had a guard there.

"We want to go for a drink," Jake said to the guard. "Get off the ship and walk around for a while."

"No problem," replied the guard. "But if you start a fight, it won't go well for you."

"No problems. We just need a break."

Jake took the directions to the bar, which, as he predicted, was not far from the base of the truss.

"They don't want strangers going too far into the station," he said as they walked down the corridor.

The bar had beer taps down one side, stand-up tables around the others, and a few metal tables with metal chairs bolted down in the back. Jake walked up to the bartender.

"We'd like four beers and four super potato specials. How much will that be in GG credits?"

"Do you have glasses and cutlery?" the bartender asked.

"Not with us," Jake said, exaggerating his accent.

The bartender nodded. "Eighteen credits all in, then."

Jake handed him a twenty-credit chip and let him keep the extra as a tip.

"Thanks. What are you folks here for?"

"This and that. Buying and selling."

"What are you buying and selling?"

"We're looking for metals. We have a few things to sell, but mostly we're buying. Know anybody with platinum? Or rhodium and ruthenium?"

"Not offhand. But who knows who might pass through?"

"Who does, indeed. We'll take that table over there?"

"Surely. I'll bring the beers over."

The group walked to the table. Suzanne sat with her back to the wall. Jake sat beside her, while Zeke and Vidal sat in front of them. Suzanne kept her gun hand clear. She looked very alert, and was scanning the room from side to side. Where had she learned that? Vidal? Jake didn't want to think about that, so he tried to focus back on the task at hand. She had begun to treat Jake as a confusing combination of schoolteacher and potential boyfriend. When she had technical questions, she asked him and quizzed him quite seriously, but outside of that she kept up a low level of flirting that drove Jake insane.

The waitress arrived shortly after they sat, and Jake had the same conversation with her as the bartender, but she was more direct. "Wait here. I'll send some friends."

Jake nodded. The bartender was making and taking calls on a hardphone between pouring drinks. People were starting to arrive in the bar and sit together, and they stared at the three Petrel crewmembers. They muttered to each other, and on some secret signal, one older man sauntered over and pulled up an empty chair between Zeke and Vidal.

"I'm Helmut."

"Jake."

"I hear you want to buy metal?"

"Yes. I have GG credits."

"I hear you paid a pretty penny to the station office."

"We traded a pretty penny. Credit deals are for less. You know that."

"How much less?"

"I'll pay five hundred a kilogram for platinum or palladium, seven-fifty for iridium, and a thousand for the Rs."

"That's way less than you paid at the office."

"That was a bulk transaction. It was refined and packaged, and we didn't pay credit. We traded. That's what we pay. You want to do a deal or not?"

Helmut reached into a pocket and Suzanne sat forward, reaching for her weapon. She didn't relax until Helmut produced an ingot from his pocket. He hadn't noticed Suzanne's movement.

"Five hundred grams of mixed. Twenty-five percent silver, 25 percent iridium, and the rest is the Rs."

Jake took a small kit out of his pocket. He weighted the bar and used a laser to find its volume, then he shined a bright light on it and reflected it to a sensor.

"Not quite, but close. I'll give you a hundred for it."

"Four hundred."

"One-twenty."

They bickered back and forth for a minute but soon settled on a price. The man was pleased, and Jake could tell he had overpaid. He made a mental note to adjust his bids with the next taker. For the next hour, a constant stream of arrivals came to the table. Jake bought almost ten kilograms of various mixed metals.

After some time, Vidal stood up. "Stewart, you seem to be doing an adequate enough job. I've got to supervise an engineering refit on the winches. I'll want a full report, with amounts and credit values. No cheating me or I'll find out."

"Of course not, sir," said Jake.

"LaFleur, you're with me," Vidal said, nodding his head at Zeke. Zeke stood and gave Jake a wink as he walked after Vidal.

Jake looked over at Suzanne, who was signaling to the bartender for another round. They were alone together, but Jake couldn't find anything to say.

"Jake, you are a strange one," she said, after a few quiet moments.

"How so?"

"You are worried that Bassi would know if you cheated, are you not?"

"Yes."

"But of course, he will not. You have been buying and selling and trading for an hour. Does he know how much you have bought or sold? He does not. You bought some gold. You sold gold. You traded gold for silver. Why did you do that?"

"Gold bars are too big for regular expenses, but silver is fine. They were in five-gram bars, perfect for locals to buy and sell. I knew it would be easier to get rid of them. And when I want to buy small amounts of ore, silver will be better."

"See? You knew that. He did not. You can pocket half of what we have here and nobody will ever know."

"I wouldn't do that."

"No. No, you would not. We know that. He is not worried. He wants to make you worry."

The waitress dropped the new beers off. "Shift change in thirty minutes. You should stay. My sister will be coming on shift. She'd like to talk to you."

Jake and Suzanne settled in. Jake scanned the bar. He noticed it was much fuller than when they'd arrived. They had injected a lot of new currency into this station's economy, and people were spending it.

Jake bought and sold, sold and bought. His pile of PGMs grew relative to his other metals, and he retained small amounts of credits and other currency.

Jake had just bought ten grams of metal off a boy who looked about seven, when Suzanne sat up straight and gripped his arm with her left hand. Her right snapped to her holster.

"Jake, we have a problem."

"How so?"

"That man at the far table, with the toolbelt. He and a friend have been here for an hour, watching us and nursing their drinks. That package—I just got a glimpse, another man came in and gave it to them. He just gave each of them a knife, which they hid down their pants. The other went outside. I can see him waiting in the corridor."

"Knives? Are you sure?"

Suzanne surveyed the bar and the entrance. "Jake, we are in danger. We need to move, and we need to move now. Rush past the first one, bash the second one, and run for the ship."

"How are we in danger? What is going to happen?"

"We will take them by surprise."

"Surprise? They have knives. Suzanne, what are you talking about?"

"Jake," Suzanne said. She paused for a moment and collected herself. She removed her hand from his arm, but turned his face towards her. "Jake, mon ami, please. Do as I ask. As a favor to me." She grinned at him. The grin was like kryptonite to Jake. He started packing the metals and currency into his satchel.

"They will try to get us out of the bar to ambush," Suzanne said.

"Suzanne, where did you learn about knives and ambushes?"

She ignored the question. "Jake, you know stations. They want somewhere narrow and quiet where we cannot run away. Where would that be?"

"They won't attack in the loading dock. That's too

likely to be monitored. But the corridors from there to there probably don't have cameras or anything."

"Yes, I agree. We need a diversion here in the bar, then you charge the small one there and run out the door. I will take care of the other while you make your way to the ship."

Jake looked at her in surprise. "I can't just leave you behind."

"Do not worry, Jake," Suzanne said, smiling. Jake had seen the same smile on Zeke when he did something crazy. "I will be fine. I will be right behind you."

Jake finished packing things up into his carry satchel, and into the various pockets he had on his suit. The expensive metals—the rhodium and ruthenium—went into an internal, sealed, zippered pocket. The cheaper stuff, including a double handful of copper slugs that he had taken in trade, went into an outer pocket.

"Now we need a diversion," Suzanne said.

"That I can help with," Jake said. He waved the waitress over.

"I would like to buy a beer for everybody in the bar to say thank-you. You folks can set them all up and announce it. Here's . . . fifty credits. That should be enough for the beers and something for you as well."

"It sure is. Thanks, mister. Free trades." She hustled back behind the bar and spoke to the bartender. He nodded and began to fill a tray of the smallest glasses with the cheapest beer. He filled two large trays before standing on the bar, right beside the men with knives.

"A round of BB courtesy of the gentleman in the corner! Free trades! Stay put, Lai will bring it out."

"Free trades!" The room erupted in cheering and many people stood up and saluted Jake with their existing drinks. Jake stood, nodded and raised his glass at the crowd in general. He put hand on Suzanne's shoulder and bent down to talk to her.

"Don't get up yet, but be ready to move," he said.

Suzanne nodded. She slid to the edge of her chair, poised to run.

Jake stepped up on his chair. The waitress had just about finished serving everybody. There were twice as many beer glasses on the tables as there had been a minute ago. The room quieted as he got up.

"Thank you, everyone." Jake removed his hand from a pocket on his suit. It was full of small silver coins. He began to pour them from hand to hand where everybody could see them. It was a big handful, there were lots of coins, and they gleamed in the low light.

"Thanks everybody. Free trades!"

"Free trades," the crowd shouted.

"And, as is traditional—lucky strikes to everybody!" Jake yelled, and threw the handful of coins out into the crowd.

The room went wild. Coins rained out over the room, landing on tables, the floor, splashing in glasses, sticking to clothes. Jake had aimed the bulk of them towards where the knife man was sitting.

The crowd rushed the corner where he sat, forming a pushing, shoving mass as they scrabbled for the coins. Inevitably some beer was spilled and people got pushed around. Some pushed back and a few minor tussles erupted, adding to the confusion.

Jake jumped down and dashed across the room, past the bemused bartender toward the door. He banged into one of the men on the way, knocking him into a table of people. Then he skidded towards the exit. Suzanne boomed past and bounced off the far wall before correcting herself and turning right down the hallway.

Someone pushed into Jake and he nearly tripped, but he righted his step and took off through the door. He swung round the corner and pivoted down the hallway. He pounded down the corridor, bouncing from floor to ceiling and back, racing for a T-junction and a closed airlock ahead of him.

A man in coveralls with a toolbelt came around the corner. Jake realized he didn't know what their opponents looked like. Suzanne did, because she whooped and dove for the man. She drove headfirst into his shoulder. He went down, and she flipped over him and managed to hit the locking wheel feet-first. She had become much better in low-G. Suzanne bounced back up onto her feet, and rolled around the corner and down the corridor. She looked a little worse for wear, bouncing from one side to another in a sort of shambling run. Some of her hair had come loose from her ponytail.

"Jake, I think if we take this corridor anti-spinward and take the next spar rimward, we'll come to the outer ring, and we can run back to the ship that way," she yelled.

"You're right, let's go."

They ran forward. Jake steadied Suzanne so she wouldn't pinball off the walls, and slowed them down to a steady high-speed shuffle. They kept moving down the corridor for a minute. The Petrel shouldn't be too far away now, but why was the corridor so empty?

"Suzanne, something's wrong. There should have been another spar by now. One is missing."

"Are you sure?"

"Yes."

"Well, should we go back the way we came, and meet l'ami with the knife?"

"Good point. That way," Jake said. He pointed forward.

They kept moving, but at a slower pace. Jake stopped.

"Suzanne, where is everybody?"

"What do you mean?" Suzanne asked.

"This is a working station. There should be people here. Where are they?"

"Busy working?"

"There should be more and more people as we get closer to the docks. But this area looks deserted."

They heard voices behind them. At least two, maybe

more. Suzanne spun around and raised her eyebrows at Jake. Two men appeared in the distance. They were brandishing shiny things that, from a distance, looked an awful lot like blades.

Jake spied a truss with a set of stairs ahead of them.

"Down the truss stairs," Jake said. They began to descend.

Jake heard a shout ahead of them.

Like all stations, this one provided the feeling of gravity by spinning. When you walked "around" a level, you were actually being pushed into the floor by the spin. It was like spinning a hula hoop and walking on the inside edge. When you moved within a spinning ring from the hub to the rim, you either climbed up to the hub or down to the rim via either a ladder or stairs.

This truss had stairs. Suzanne and Jake clattered down them, bouncing a bit in the low gravity. They could hear the group behind them, gaining on them. Suzanne stopped and mounted the railing.

"Bien, Jake. It will be faster if we just drop. We can catch one of the railings at a lower level. The gravity is not large."

"No!" Jake reached out and yanked Suzanne back. "Gravity gets stronger as we get farther away from the hub. If you drop off the edge, you'll go slow at first but then faster and faster the farther out you get. Soon you'll be going too fast to stop yourself."

"Really?" Suzanne said, getting down from the railing.

"Yes, come on. We need to keep going." They clattered down the stairs. As Jake had predicted, the gravity got stronger. They ran down to the bottom. Suzanne stopped and drew her gun. Jake stopped as well. This was not a regular docking truss. It was a dead end. There were no connecting tubes or rings. It ended in two airlocks: one for cargo, one for people.

"Jake, what happens now?" Suzanne said.

"Not sure."

"You should try the comm," Suzanne said.

He spoke into it, frowned, keyed it again, and spoke louder.

"Why are they not answering?" Suzanne said.

"I'm not surprised. We're too far inside and there is too much metal around us for direct connections. We've been using repeaters."

"Then they have hacked into the repeaters?"

Jake shook his head. "It's their equipment. They would have a friend in the station who would turn it off for them or for the ship. That's what I would do."

A voice yelled from above.

"Hey, traders. We just want the gold and platinum. Toss it up and we'll leave you alone."

A head appeared around the top of the stairs. Suzanne aimed carefully and shot at him. She was rewarded by a pinging sound and a poof of dust as the bullet spent itself on the stairs. The head disappeared.

"No need to be like that," the voice said. "If you're reasonable, we will be too. We'll just take what we want and be on our way. No hard feelings."

"They'll take our money, our suits, and then push us out the nearest airlock," Jake said.

"If you come down here, I will shoot you," Suzanne yelled up the stairs and fired again. She flipped the cylinder of her revolver out and began pulling bullets out.

"With ship bullets? That might hurt, but we can take it."

"Can you take this?" Suzanne asked, then aimed and pulled the trigger. This time there was a pinging sound, and Jake heard the bullet ricochet off a girder.

"Solids," the voice said. "Well played. But you're not the only one with a real weapon." There was a ratcheting sound that Jake associated with a shotgun. "And you only have six shots in that beast, and there are four of us. And Sanjay is pretty pissed at you for slamming him into that lock, so he is going to collect some mining shields. If we have to go hard, it will go hard for you."

"What's a mining shield?" Suzanne whispered.

"Big metal plate with a handle. Used to keep boiling metal from condensing on you and as protection when you're using explosives to break rock."

"Will it stop solids?"

"Not sure. Probably."

The voice spoke again. "So, you've got five minutes to sort yourself out and toss the money up. But when Sanjay gets here, all bets are off."

Suzanne kept her attention up the stairs. The men, or rather people—they could hear at least one female voice—were hidden around a bend. They couldn't show themselves to fire the shotgun, or Suzanne would have a shot. But Suzanne couldn't very well just hike up there without getting shot herself. Jake looked around the landing they were on. There was nothing, no tools, just the airlock. Two airlocks, actually: a personnel one and a cargo one. He flipped the personnel hatch open and looked inside. Nothing there.

"Jake, we have our suits and helmets. Can't we just dive out the airlock, and the station will spin away below us?"

"That's not how it works. The station is spinning. If we hop out the airlock, we'll still have some of that spin. We'll float away from the station into space, just at an angle. They will shoot us."

"Oh. We are stuck here?"

Jake had been staring through the cargo airlock window. It was a big one. What was that in the corner?

"Maybe not," Jake said, smiling. "Into the lock. I have a plan."

Jake fussed over the controls of the outer door of the cargo lock, then got it grinding open. He ran back to the floor, which was descending, and hopped on the broomstick that he had pulled off the wall. The

141

broomstick was a metal truss with seats, a mesh cargo box on the front, and an engine on the back. The engine combined O and H and blasted the resulting vapor out the back. There were simple aspect jets attached on the back. They had no life support or communication equipment. Just the motor, jets, and metal.

"Let's go," Suzanne said, hopping behind Jake as he did up the seatbelt.

"How much do you weigh?" Jake asked as Suzanne placed an arm around his waist.

"What?"

"How much do you weigh?"

"Jake, this is not the time."

"I need to know your mass—I'm trying to figure out how much margin we have with this engine."

"Seventy-five kilograms."

Jake was silent. That was heavy for a girl, even a tall one. He calculated how much fuel he had.

Suzanne misunderstood his silence. She took the revolver and placed it against his thigh. "If you tell me that I need to lose weight, I will shoot you. It's all muscle. Let's go."

"Suzanne, it's not that simple. We're being flung away from the station at a regular rate, so we need to counteract that to stay in place and head inward a little bit. The ship will spin around to where we are, but we have to counteract the force to get there, and we have to decelerate when we see them, and given our maximum thrust. . . ."

The personnel airlock next to them began to drop, and a head stuck out, followed by a shotgun.

"Jake, shut up and drive," Suzanne yelled.

Jake pulled the throttle and they were off.

Jake immediately realized he was in trouble. He needed to steer counter to the rotation of the station to get to their ship, but that meant the station was spinning toward him at high speed. He pointed the broomstick forward and aimed directly for the next truss. He also had yellow lights on fuel for both the main engines and the aspect jets.

He pivoted the broomstick up, just a touch, and gave a bit more thrust, so that he'd just clear the mass of girders, then rolled the broomstick to the left and punched the thrust. They just skimmed by the giant ore barge that had been attached to the top of the truss.

"Jake, are you trying to kill us?" Suzanne yelled over their local channel.

"We don't have enough fuel to go around things. We have to go through them."

Jake waited till they were clear, then reversed the maneuvers, steering back toward the middle of the next truss.

"What are you doing?"

"I have to cancel out every move I make, otherwise we'll just fly by the Petrel at full speed."

Jake gave them a touch more downspin and looked ahead to judge his next move.

As they skimmed by the next truss, Jake saw a blue spot streak past them and then sparks on the girder ahead of him. What was that?

"Jake, they are shooting at us."

"I see that."

Suzanne squirmed around and tried to point her arm backward but couldn't manage it. "I do not have a shot."

"Hang on," Jake said.

Using the aspect jets, he pivoted the broomstick around so that it was flying backwards. Suzanne now had a clear view behind her. They could see two broomsticks. There were two figures on each, a driver and a shooter. One had a shotgun, the other a revolver. Jake looked down at his board. The aspect jets had changed to red. He had very little fuel left. They would have to stay pointing this way.

Suzanne pointed at the nearest one and began to shoot. Nothing happened.

"Why am I missing them?" she said over the private

channel.

Jake had turned and was trying to maneuver the broomstick backwards. He turned his head to look at his pursuers.

"They're corkscrewing, see. They give a quick puff every second or so, then back again. You'll never hit them with that random movement that far away. Save your ammo until we're close to the Petrel. We'll have to slow all the way down to dock with it."

"Damn," she said. "It is too bad you could not disable that other airlock to keep them from chasing us."

Jake felt himself blush inside his suit. He had forgotten his toolkit in his thigh pocket. He could have disabled the lock with no trouble. He had panicked and forgotten.

"Yeah, too bad," he said.

Jake pitched the nose up and gave a spurt on the main engine to clear the next truss.

"Shit," he yelled as he looked back over his shoulder. He had driven them up above the truss all right—right into another ore barge winching containers back and forth from the station. He pivoted the broomstick forward so he could get a better view of obstacles. Chains seemed to be everywhere. He pivoted left and right, and then stood the broomstick on its end, relative to their trajectory, and spurted it just above the second-to-last chain.

He would have made it, too, but he forgot about the basket in the front. It clipped a chain, and the broomstick began to rapidly pivot end over end over end.

"Jake, make it stop."

Jake looked down. The aspect jet was flashing red. Fuel exhaustion imminent.

"I can't."

"What?"

"We don't have enough fuel for the jets. And we're still going in the right direction."

Jake watched the horizon spin around. Front truss, space, pursuers, back truss, more space, front truss. One of the pursuers was burning perpendicular to their course, going "up high." A stuck engine or loss of nerve, it didn't matter. They were out of the fight.

Jake craned his neck. Another truss was approaching. He recognized it.

"The Petrel is on the next one past this truss," he said to Suzanne.

"What do we do? Can we stop this spinning?"

"I'll try. But I don't have much fuel, and I need it for deceleration."

He began to apply gentle puffs of the aspect jets, slowing down the spin. He also pulsed the main engine as they spun around. He needed to be able to point the engine opposite their trajectory to slow them down enough, otherwise they would scream past their ship without stopping.

Or splatter against the hull like an ice asteroid.

"Jake, they are gaining on us."

"I know, but I have to slow down."

"I have only a few shots left, and I'll never hit them spinning like this. Can't we throw something at them?"

"I don't have anything. Wait."

Jake reached down to one of his suit's many pockets. Was it still there, even after all the running and spinning?

It was. The handful of copper ingots he had taken in trade. He looked over his shoulder. They were approaching the Petrel. At long last, some luck was with them—they were in line with it. In fact, they would impact just aft of the airlock on a container painted bright blue, labeled "Sunshine Moving." Jake took a quick look back. He firewalled the aspect jets, slowing their spin, then fired the main engine to slow them as much as he could, waited for the right moment, and threw the handful of copper slugs up and sideways. Then he pivoted and drove the broomstick down toward the ship.

The pursuers pivoted their broomsticks and the back figure pointed the shotgun at them. Then the driver saw the copper glinting in front of him. Not knowing what it was, he began evasive maneuvers to avoid it, pouring on the lateral thrust to bypass it. But they could only thrust one direction at a time, so they had no opportunity to dump velocity as they screamed by the ship.

Jake firewalled the aspect jets and managed to reduce their spin quite a bit before they just stopped working. No fuel. They would keep spinning for now. They were moving in the correct direction but pivoting end over end. Every rotation they spun around to see the giant "Sunshine Moving" symbol getting bigger and bigger. Jake pulsed the throttle when they were pointing in the right direction. Now the main engine light was flashing red. It was going to be close.

Too close.

"Suzanne, point the gun straight up. When I say fire, shoot the gun."

"What?"

"We need to stop the spin so I can fire the main engine. Ready?"

"Ready."

"Wait, wait, three, two, one and half, a quarter, SHOOT!"

Suzanne fired just as the engine pointed back at the ship. Their spinning slowed almost to a stop. Jake waited for spin to settle, then firewalled the throttle and looked back over his shoulder. It helped—they were slowing relative to the ship. Slowing, slowing.

The main engine failed. Crap.

Jake watched helplessly as they floated toward the ship. They were not moving fast, but fast enough that they would break an arm or a leg or a neck and bounce off the ship into the void.

Suzanne was fumbling at her belt, pulling bullets out.

"Sorry, Suzanne," Jake said. Damn.

She didn't say anything but finished reloading. Then she twisted to one side and began firing her revolver. One at a time, she fired directly into the center of the giant green "Sunshine Moving" sign.

Jake counted the shots. One, two, they were slowing. Three, four, very slow. Five, almost stopped.

Suzanne held her fire until they had drifted within a meter of the Petrel, then fired her last round directly at the center of the green sign. It vanished in a puff of dust, and they floated twenty centimeters away, at rest relative to the ship.

12

"Three sevens. Read 'em and weep," Nadine said. She leaned forward and scooped up her winnings, adding them to the modest pile in front of her.

The man across from her smiled and shook his head. "Good for you," he said. He tossed his two-pair into the center.

Nadine looked at him as she shuffled for the next hand. Short, dark, heavily muscular, and with a soft accent she couldn't quite identify. Yummy. She wondered if maybe she should end this game early.

They had started with six people six hours ago. Juan was the only one left. Some sort of GG mining administrator or something. The others had played well but had soon realized they were outclassed. Juan was obviously the local champ, but he was having a hard time beating Nadine. He was very good, Nadine admitted. Perhaps as good as her, but she wasn't interested in spending another six hours trying to find out how good he was at poker. Perhaps he was good at other things.

They were on a small GG satellite station, one rarely visited by merchant ships. They were required to trade only with a larger GG station in the neighborhood. Sell everything there, buy everything from it. And at ruinous prices. The staff at this station were not enthused with that arrangement and had greeted her ship and supplies with open arms. After they had bought all the PGMs for sale, Nadine had declared a twelve-hour break and broke out their most expensive food trays and a bottle of cider. Demitrios didn't drink. Sue only weighed about fifty kilograms, and because she was of Earth-Asian ancestry, alcohol consumption made her break out in hives. They had locked the ship down and gone gratefully to sleep a full shift ago.

Nadine had headed to the bar and offered to share her cider with the card players. They had accepted, and gave her all types of useful intelligence—economic, navigational, and personal. She had a whole list of stations to visit and a good idea of which ones had not seen a ship in months, which ones welcomed strange traders, and which ones would cause trouble.

Her comm beeped. She frowned. That would only happen if an alarm had woken Sue or Big D.

"Yes?"

"Problem," Sue said. "Big ship just showed up on our sensors."

"How big?"

"Hard to be sure. Three, four times our size at least."

"Militia?"

"Doubt it. Unless cutters regularly boost at .3 G. But it's coming this way, and it's big enough to have weapons. We should drop."

"On my way," Nadine said. She looked at her companion. Her exploration of everything he was good at would have to wait for another time.

"Ship's coming. Any idea who it might be?"

"Yes, it is the Bountiful Onion. They were scheduled to arrive sometime soon. It is not very fast but it is large. And it is armed. It is best you be gone before they get here."

"What about you? Will you get into trouble?"

"Us? What trouble? You did not dock here, just sailed by on your way elsewhere. You are not a GG ship. We do not know anything about you."

Nadine laughed. "Here, take this," she said, shoving the cider toward him.

"Thank you. Perhaps we will share it again, some other time."

***

"What is that infernal bonging noise?" Captain Marchello said, entering the bridge.

Everyone looked at the first officer, who was quickly vacating the command chair.

"That is the general quarters alarm, captain," he said. "I'm sure it sounded different on your other ships."

"Yes, yes, of course," Captain Marchello said. "What is happening?"

The helmsman blinked and opened his mouth. "Shouldn't it be the same on all ships—?"

"Watch your course, helm," said the first officer, looking down and shaking his head. "The captain has no time for your yapping. Captain, we have detected a ship on radar in the vicinity of the station. It is not responding to hails, and its beacon is not lit. It's a modified freighter of some kind, but none of its type are assigned to this route."

"I see. Pirates. Well, let's pursue her."

"Of course. We will go to full acceleration. Helm, calculate when we will overtake her."

The helmsman looked up at the first officer. "Overtake her?" he whispered.

Again, the first officer shook his head. The other ship was already pulling 2 G or more. The Bountiful Onion could only go up to .5 G, and things might fall off then. Even from a running start, they wouldn't catch the other ship. The helmsman put the numbers into the computer and ran the calculations anyways. After a minute, the answer came back.

"Sir, the computer says that due to the spatial geometry of the two ships, we do not have an intercept course."

"Your orders, captain," said the first officer.

The captain pondered. His chess game with the doctor had been interrupted, and that was irritating. These people, whoever they were, should be punished.

"Bring us into weapons range, then. Prepare the mass driver. We will teach these people a lesson."

The first officer had a vision of them starting the first true inter-corporate war in Delta's history. Just because the ship didn't answer with a corporate beacon didn't mean it wasn't a corporate ship.

The gunner at his console cleared his throat. "Right away, captain. Umm, we will need to divert water resources to cool the mass driver. Should I divert the water for your sauna and shower or the crew's drinking water?"

The first officer shot the gunner a significant look. He worried that the captain might decide to doom the crew to death by dehydration, provided he still got his daily sauna.

The captain shook his head. "Never mind, let them go. Take us in to the station." The captain stalked off the bridge.

The first officer let out a breath. "Thank the Emperor he didn't remember we have lasers as well," the gunner said. The first officer stifled a laugh.

***

"Well done, LaFleur. Suzanne, I'm impressed by that shooting thing at the end. Showed clear thinking under fire," Vidal said. He smiled at Suzanne as he said it. Jake grimaced.

"It was nothing, Bassi." She smiled back and placed her hand on Vidal's arm.

Jake cleared his throat. "I'm fine as well, sir."

Vidal looked at him. "Yes. Ah, good driving, Stewart." Vidal turned and walked away.

Suzanne's eyes followed him as he left. Jake wasn't happy to see that look.

Vidal stopped and turned. "Stewart."

"Yes sir?"

"You've done well, despite yourself. You may have your comm privileges back. For now." Vidal turned back and walked away.

Jake jumped as Zeke came up behind him and thumped his shoulder.

"Great work, Jake. Thanks for saving my sister."

"Well, Suzanne sort of saved herself. She's a pretty good shot."

"Yes, yes she is. But it's a good thing you are a much better driver than a shooter, no?"

"Sure. Thanks, Zeke."

"Why, even Vidal thinks that you did well. Come, eat with us. I bought some beer on-station. We can share."

"Thanks, Zeke."

"How did you get to be such a good driver of a broomstick, Jake?" Zeke asked as they walked over to the mess table in the middle of the deck.

"I'm not that good. I was trained on one when I was young, and we had to use it all the time at my station. It just takes practice, as you know. You've gotten much better yourself."

"Yes, I have been practicing whenever we have a break at a station."

"You are lucky. I am jealous," Suzanne said. "I wish I had your talent for flying. Perhaps I will ask Bassi to show me how to fly a broomstick next."

"Well, I wish I had your talent with a gun. You never miss."

"I'm just lucky."

"Enough about talent," Zeke said. "Time to celebrate."

Zeke opened a beer and passed it to Jake before opening one for himself.

"Don't let Jake drink too much, Zeke. We all know what happens then." Suzanne walked over to Jake.

She started to walk away, then stopped, turned back, and leaned in close. He was startled but didn't move away. He could smell her cologne. "Oh, and Jake," she said, whispering close to his ear. "Thank you again for saving me." She put her hands on his shoulders and kissed him very firmly on the lips, holding it for a long time. Jake froze. After what seemed like forever, she pushed back, smiled, and turned and walked toward the ladder toward Vidal's office. "See you boys in the morning."

**

"That was too close. They could have shot us up," said Sue.

"Yes," said Nadine, "this has got to stop." She turned off the audio alarm of the radar receiver. It had been beeping since the large cargo ship had appeared in the distance heading toward the station.

"Let's get a look at her," Nadine said, switching to the telescope. They didn't have much in the way of active sensors—no masers, for example, but they had good passive ones.

"Big," Nadine said. "Thousand tons, maybe. Interior cargo bays and lots of truss space."

"That's a laser on the top," Sue said.

"And two more on the sides," said Nadine.

"What's that on the bottom?"

"That's a mass driver. A rail gun." Nadine switched back to the pilot's screen and inserted a few random course changes and a couple of random thrust changes as well.

"What's that for?" Sue asked.

"If they shoot that mass driver at us, they usually shoot

where they think we'll be based on our vector at the time of shooting. We just need a slight change to move out of their perceived path. They can almost never hit ships."

"What's the use of a rail gun over a laser, then?"

"I said almost never, not never. And when they hit, the kinetic energy causes much more damage than a laser. And they're deadly against stations or anything that can't dodge, like an unpowered satellite."

"Where to next?"

"We've been following the TGI playbook, running along those GG colonies. We need to think outside the box, or outside of the regular trade routes, anyway. Take over for a while. I'm going to do some research."

***

"Platinum group. Sure, we have lots. Come on down," said the voice on the radio. "We'll do some trading. Whatever you need."

Nadine and Sue looked at each other. They'd headed away from the regular routes, moving instead toward a small cluster of stations and proto-stations that were not members of any corporate grouping or route.

Pirate stations, most probably.

"You think they have anything? Or are they just getting us down there to rob us?" Sue asked.

"Both, I think. I'm sure they have some PGMs."

"How do you know?"

"Part of a container load went missing out this way about a year back. It probably ended up here."

"Again, how do you know?"

"Some gambling friends told me." Nadine shrugged as she spun the ship to face the "station" on the asteroid.

"That's not even a station. That's a bunch of containers landed and connected by access tubes. What's that in the middle?"

"Looks like a junked ship. That will be their fusion

plant."

"This place looks sketchy, Nadine."

"It does. And just in case, we'll take some insurance." Nadine flicked the comm. "Big D, bring the blue banded gun case from the ship's locker and meet me at the airlock. Don't try to open it."

"Or it will explode?" the voice across the comm asked.

"No, this one releases deadly gas. Just bring it and don't open it. We're going to go Old Empire on these guys."

The station airlock door swung inward, then stuck. Nadine had to lean her shoulder into it to get it moving again, and then it stuck again. She stepped forward and pushed it with both hands, walking it open.

The area inside was dark, with just an emergency light visible. Nadine could see a vague figure under it, but nothing else. She looked around. "Chin? Are you Chin?"

"Go," a voice said. Three spotlights flooded the compartment, catching Nadine and her party in a harsh glare. Nadine put her hand over her forehead, shielding her eyes against the light.

"Freeze. Drop your weapons, or we'll shoot."

"No way," Nadine said. "You freeze and drop your weapons, or we'll shoot. And get that light out of my eyes."

The voice paused, coughed once. "That's not the way it works."

"Listen, you've got, at best, a couple folks with revolvers. You might have a shotgun with solid slugs in it, but that's all. You need our ship undamaged, so you don't dare fire into it. We, on the other hand, have full hard suits on and we're not firing ship ammo, because I don't give a crap if your low-rent habitat ends up leaking atmo from five hundred holes."

"I don't believe you."

"There better be nothing important behind that light

up there," Nadine said, pointing up toward the ceiling, "because I'm going to make it go away."

She barely twitched her finger, and suddenly there was a soft crack and the light exploded.

"So, you shot a light out. Big deal," Chin said. He coughed again.

"I also blew out the fixture and shot a hole in the wall, probably melting it. If you check the next few walls behind that, probably them as well. It likely went all the way through this ship and out the other side. You're losing atmo as we speak."

Nadine waited. A second later the alarm started bonging in the distance.

"Perfect timing. Big D, lights."

Lights came on behind Nadine. Big D stood behind her carrying a strange-looking rifle. The barrel was surrounded by a thick coil of wire, and a bright spotlight was attached. She saw four figures in front of her. Two pointed revolvers at her. Chin was short, with black hair and yellowish skin. He had no weapon in his hands, but he did have a big handkerchief that he pressed to a runny nose.

"Ever seen one of these?" Nadine asked, turning her hand slightly so Chin and the others could see what she was holding.

It was a small gun, but very odd-looking. There was no obvious barrel, just two parallel metal rails with a coil around them connected to an almost rectangular handgrip with a button on top.

"I have," said a new voice from behind a revolver. "Not in real life, but I seen pictures. Is that a gauss gun?"

"Full points to you," Nadine said. "The finest the Old Empire could produce. Now put down your weapons."

"What's a gauss gun?" Chin asked.

"Big magnets, small metal needles, high velocity. Shoots ten gram needles at three kilometers per second. The velocity makes up for the size. It'll punch through any armor and walls, and it fires at full automatic as long as I keep the trigger down. Oh, and it's keyed to my fingerprint, so you can't use it."

"It's just one gun," Chin said.

"I have one, Sue has one, Big D back there has its big brother, and we're wearing armor. Throw your guns down or we'll have the shootout and see who comes off best."

One of the shadows coughed, shrugged, and holstered his weapon. The others did the same.

"Now," Nadine said, "let's do some trading."

***

"That wasn't what I expected," Sue said.

"How so?"

"For a pirate base, it was really poor."

"Not much money in pirating, especially if you have nowhere to sell your booty."

"Booty?"

"That's what it's called. Booty. The stuff they steal."

"Where do they get 'booty' from?" Sue said as she stifled a cough.

"They'll have a small ship, perhaps two. They raid settlements or ships, and sometimes they'll go into a bigger station and trade."

"Where's the ship now?"

"Off somewhere, I guess. I think they were a little worried. Notice they bought food and medical stuff, and only the one set of handguns. Their ship might be overdue."

Sue coughed again. "It was pretty dumpy, really. Broken-down ship, old furniture. It seemed to be a collection of things that people threw out into the trash."

"It probably was. What were you expecting? Jewels? Rich food? Banquets?"

"And served by handsome muscular waiters with their shirts off, if the vids are anything to go by."

"Welcome to reality."

"Where to now?"

"We're heading to the biggest station in this cluster here. It's the center of a group of mining stations—a few free-floating stations, some iceworks, a bunch of stuff. Even has its own foundry and a mill. A small one."

"What's it called?"

"Roundhouse."

***

"We're trying something new this time," Vidal said.

"Is that why we've been under acceleration for a whole day?" Zeke asked.

"Yes. As much as I hate to admit it, Stewart has done a good job. Now we're after just the high-value metals. We've picked up word of a new set of pseudo colonies— the Roundhouse. They're a little off the beaten path, but hopefully that will mean they'll have a stockpile of metals to trade with us. We're going to hit them up, let Stewart do his thing, and head out of here. If we do this right, we can all go home early. We do this right, and I'll let the Militia know you've served your sentence. You get me what I need, and you'll all be free by the time this is over."

Everybody smiled at this.

"And I'll get my regular crew back," Vidal said.

Aha, Jake thought. Vidal couldn't ask for replacements while they were still on board, but he could have them freed, and get his old partners in crime back.

"We'll have to spend at least two days at the station," Vidal continued. "We'll need to shut the drive down to do maintenance, and the nav crew will need a break. I'll need to supervise here on ship, so you three will be on your own for the trade. This is a family-run place and they have a good reputation, so I'm not worried. But wear revolvers, just in case. Not you, Jake."

Jake nodded. He had assumed that.

"Once your work is done, if you get everything we need, you can take some leave. Jake, either you or Zeke have to stay on the ship. You two work it out."

Jake thought for a moment. If Suzanne was off the ship on the station . . . and so was he, some things might . . . improve.

Zeke spoke for both of them. "Jake and I will work it out, sir." He winked at Jake. "We will do some trading, yes."

Jake nodded agreement. He was good at trading.

Jake trooped out of the lock with Zeke and Suzanne. The airlock and truss weren't large, but there were three other ships docked at the same time, all smaller than the Petrel.

"For a station this small, they sure have a lot of visitors," Jake said as they walked down the corridor to meet their contact.

A tall, white-haired man who was wearing some sort of robe and a tooled leather belt with a revolver holstered to it met them on board the station.

"Welcome, I am Elder Davi. Which one of you is Mr. Stewart?"

"I am," Jake said.

"Welcome. I have reviewed the list of metals you sent and your suggestions on prices. I don't agree with the prices, of course," he flashed a smile at Jake, "but we can talk about things in my office."

"Of course."

They proceeded down the tube and arrived at an inner ring and entered a large storage area. Rather than chairs, the wall had metal benches. The four of them sat.

"I will tell you honestly, Mr. Stewart, that I would like to have our business here concluded quickly, even though that gives you an advantage."

"Why so?"

"It is our three-year clan gathering."

"I see. I was curious as to why you had so many ships docked. We'll not take up too much of your time."

"What is a clan gathering, Jake?" Zeke interrupted.

Jake tried to wave him off but Elder Davi seemed glad to answer.

"We're in orbital resonance with a number of other stations of the clan, and we come together every three years, with each clan station taking turns to host a gathering. We have several marriage ceremonies taking place today. My great-niece is one, and a second cousin another. There will be a celebration and meal to follow. As guests, you are invited to come and join our revelry."

"We thank you, Elder Davi. We will not keep you from your important duties. If you agree to our prices as written, we can conclude our business now."

Elder Davi laughed. "Good try. We have the metals you seek and will trade for them, but I notice you did not include fuel in your requirements."

"We have bladders, and several of our existing containers have been reconfigured as long-range fuel tanks."

"A pity. Our fuel prices are extremely reasonable. We are absolutely swimming in water-ice asteroids, and we have our own distillery and water cracker. It's solar powered, so we can run it continuously."

"You have liquid H, O, and distilled water?" Jake was surprised.

"At very reasonable prices. And if you want to reclaim some cargo space, we might trade some empty containers for those bladder-filled ones."

"I see," said Jake, intrigued. He looked at the others. "This might take a while. You should go out to the hall and mingle."

Zeke nodded. "Keep up the good work, Jake. Comm when you are ready to head back to the ship." He and Suzanne stepped out of the office door. Suzanne waved at him and followed her brother out the door.

Two days later, the Petrel dropped from the docking truss. All tanks were full. O and H topped off. Jake had two new empty containers on the hull, as the bladder-filled ones had been left chained to the truss. "Just leave them there. We'll move them after the gathering," Elder Davi had said.

Jake had a busy schedule during their stay and hadn't been able to get away. With the change from empty to full containers, they had had to re-balance the entire load, and he had spent three full shifts getting the containers relocated again.

"It's too bad you had to work so much, Jake," Zeke said, looking tired but very relaxed. "You could have spent more time on the station."

"Oh? Why so? I've seen stations like this before. Grew up on one only a little bigger, in fact."

"It wasn't the station. It was this gathering thing. The little stations send all their people over. They meet and party. Everybody was very relaxed," he said, and winked at Jake.

"So?"

"There were lots of girls, Jake. Pretty ones who only see their brothers or cousins for months. They come to these events to make new friends."

Jake had forgotten about that custom. Lack of genetic diversity was a big deal in small populations. In isolated extended families, there was sometimes a deliberate effort to expand it. And often fathers and husbands did not begrudge their daughters or wives doing their duty to expand that genetic pool.

"Did you make a new friend?" Jake asked.

"Several." Zeke stretched elaborately and yawned.

"I wouldn't have minded a new friend," Jake said.

Zeke grinned at Jake.

"Stewart." Vidal's voice rang out over the comm.

"Yes sir?" Jake said.

"Get your cargo reports together. We'll have a comm window with HQ in about an hour. I want a full report queued up before we begin our trajectory home."

"Yes sir."

"How much do you have to send?"

"Two gigabytes, sir."

"All right, stand by." There was a pause. "Okay, we're going to boost the power and run on ballistic so the bandwidth will go up. Dump everything now before we head out."

Jake understood. Orbital geometry was such that stations couldn't always see each other, so when there was a clear shot between stations they sent all their messages in a hurry. The stronger the signal, the easier it was for the receiver to read. The more detailed messages could be sent, and thus the more information per time unit. If you had a lot of information to send, you either sent it slowly at low power over a longer time and counted on error correction coding to fix any problems, or you boosted the power higher so you could send it faster. Ballistic running meant that the power from the fusion plant would be moved away from the drives to the antennas, giving a stronger signal, but the Petrel couldn't maneuver while that was happening. That was why they had to dump the communications now before they began their long trip back.

Jake worked on gathering all the necessary information for the report while Zeke relayed stories of his adventures the last two days.

"Ah, space is the life for me, Jake. And to think, when we get back, we will be free. Can you believe it?"

Jake didn't quite believe it. After all the ways he had screwed up his life, it was hard to believe that he had fixed his own mess. But it was in Vidal's own best interest to declare them free, and get back to his own stealing. And, if Jake had been reading between the lines correctly, Mr. Dashi might give him his job back for collecting the metals he needed. Yes, things might be looking up for Jake Stewart.

***

"But why aren't they maneuvering?" Sue asked.

"They don't see us," Nadine said.

"We're not invisible, Nadine. If they point a scope at us, they'll see us."

"They don't know that we're here, so they don't know where to point a scope. We're not radiating any radar or any sort of electronic sweep, so they won't know where we are. I didn't say they can't see us, just that they don't see us. If they get any idea where we are, they can hunt for us. But they aren't doing that now."

"Because of the radio signal we heard?"

"Yup. That's a very strong signal. They must be dumping a big communication to be running in ballistic. But that's good news for us."

"Why?"

"This looks like that TGI ship we heard about. The one that's been buying all the PGMs. And running in ballistic means they can't maneuver right now. I see an opportunity to finish our mission in a hurry with a little larceny."

"Don't we get shot for that?"

"Only if we get caught. Right now, they can't see anything and they can't move. They're sitting ducks. All we have to do is get in super close without being detected."

"And then?"

"Look here," Nadine said, pulling up a ship schematic on her display. "This is a standard trader layout. Everything is on their external truss. See there? Those are control feeds for the laser, and those are for the antennas. That's control for the engines and the fuel lines."

"So?"

"Hit those lines and they'll have no laser or antenna.

They won't be able to control their engines. They'll be floating in space, and we can promise to shoot the crap out of them unless they pay a ransom in PGMs."

"Nadine, this is a scout, not a warship. And that's a repurposed mining laser, not a real weapon, and our computer can barely control it."

"That's why we are going to get really close."

"A little direct, don't you think?"

"Direct can be fun."

13

Jake watched his message queue empty. There would be no acknowledgment of receipt for days, but with the message coding and redundancies in the transmission it was pretty certain that everything would get through. That appealed to his orderly mind.

He returned to listening to Zeke's chatter about what he was going to do next, now that they wouldn't be stuck in the Militia, and he suddenly started to feel sad. Zeke would most likely find a place on another ship, probably Suzanne too. Once they got back, would he ever see them again? He finally felt like he had made a real friend for the first time in a long while. He would miss Zeke.

And he would miss Suzanne. How she smelled. Maybe she would choose to stay on the Petrel. Vidal would certainly find a place for her. Jake felt his typical brooding thoughts return. He'd have to move on from Suzanne. It was clear she didn't think of him that way.

***

"Okay, here's what we're doing. Big D, you suit up and

be ready to go outside and pick up a package when we stop. Make sure that you're strapped into that webbing near the lock. I'm going to program a few course changes in ahead of time, just in case they have some sort of auto-evade or auto-fire program loaded."

"What's that?" Big D asked.

"A computer program that alters course whenever it detects a missile or mass driver firing, and fires defensive and offensive weapons."

"Do we have one of those?"

"I wish. Too expensive. I'm going to be doing weapons. Sue will be flying. But really, all that happens is, when we're close enough, fire at their laser, then their antenna, then the engine fuel lines. Then we flip and burn hard to slow down relative to them so we can get those PGMs."

"Why not shoot out the engines?"

"If we shoot out their engines, we might cause an explosion and kill people. Some of those people might be us. Also, right now we're just pirates. We can fade into the background. If we start killing whole starship crews, the Militia will send a squadron of ships to hunt us down and kill us all."

"Got it."

Nadine finished typing the course changes into the computer, then keyed the comm.

"Sue, this will be rough. You ready?"

"Ready, boss."

***

Jake tugged at his restraints as he floated in his chair. One of the advantages, or disadvantages, of ballistic flight was no acceleration-induced gravity. He watched as Zeke played with a coin in the seat beside him, watching it spin in the zero gravity. He spun it again and it drifted ever so slightly sideways.

"We just hit something," Jake said. "Something small."

"What do you mean? I did not feel anything."

A moment later the general quarters alarm sounded.

'Bong. General quarters. Bong. General quarters. Bong.'

Jake tightened his straps. Zeke did the same.

'Bong. General quarters. Bong. Stations for ship-to-ship combat. Bong.'

"Ship-to-ship combat? Jake, what is happening?" Zeke said. For the first time since Jake had met Zeke, he thought he heard fear in Zeke's voice.

The main lights went out and the emergencies came on. Jake felt a gentle sideways roll begin.

"I think we must have met some pirates," Jake responded. That was all he could think of. If that was the case, and if they were following the pirates' playbook, then the next shots would be. . . .

'Bong. Bridge control disabled. Secondary controls take over.'

That was bad. One of those shots must have cut the control lines. He felt the ship's roll grow deeper. Yup, they must have cut the control and fuel lines to the engines. The escaping fuel was acting like a thruster and rolling them.

***

"Whooohoooo!" Nadine yelled with excitement as her ship pivoted around. She kept her arms crossed across her chest, gripping the restraints as they finished their pivot. Flailing arms had been known to break fingers or wrists when they impacted a control board. When they had rotated a full 180 degrees, she found herself being pressed into the chair as the main engines fired to slow them.

She scanned her boards. "That was awesome! We got all three. No radar or comm from them, laser is down, and they're venting fuel out the back."

"Glad you like it," Sue said. She looked green and was sweating. Her nose was running, too. Some people didn't like high-G maneuvers.

"Cheer up. We'll have the PMGs on board in no time." She punched a comm. "Big D—we fly by in about a minute, then they'll gradually catch up to us. Stay sharp."

Nadine leaned back and began to count the number of oranges that she would eat. One every day? How much would that cost?

***

Jake shut the airlock hatch behind him and stood next to Zeke while he waited for the air to cycle out.

"Are you sure you don't want to wait inside, Zeke?" Jake asked.

"Jake, it will be fine. You are going to do all the work. I am just watching."

"Watching with that big rifle."

"Like Vidal said, we told them we'd have somebody armed on the hull, just in case."

"Guns make me nervous."

"You should only be frightened if the gun is pointed at you," Zeke said. "Or if you are the one holding the gun." Zeke laughed at his own joke. Jake smiled a little but tried not to show Zeke.

"Jake." Vidal's voice came through Jake's comm. "You'll need to freehand your way along the hull to find the shepherd's crook. Then you'll wait till somebody from the pirate ship shoots a line at you. Catch it, fix it to the ship, and get ready to winch a package over."

"Yes sir. I know what I'm doing."

"I don't need any lip from you, Stewart," Vidal said. "Just do this right and maybe you won't accidentally spin away to die in the void or get hit by a line, or the shepherd's crook."

The airlock finished cycling, and Jake opened the outer

door. He and Zeke climbed out.

He arrived at a spot just behind the fueling port, opened a hatch, and hefted the long metal rod with a hook at the end. He latched his safety on, then switched to the ship-to-ship hailing channel.

"This is Petrel fuel party. I mean the Petrel line party. Ready for your shot."

"Stand by, Petrel," a woman's voice replied. Odd—it sounded very familiar.

"Waiting," Jake said. He watched the other ship.

"There are two of you there. One of you has a rifle," the voice said over the comm.

"Correct."

"No rifle. That could cause problems. You have to dump it."

Jake cursed inside. It was already going sideways.

"What's the problem, you think we'll shoot you from here? With that big laser turret pointing directly at us?"

"Yes, that's exactly what I think. Dump it."

"It's too valuable to dump. What if we put it in the locker here and move away? You can see us, so if one of us goes into the locker you can blow us up or whatever."

"Good compromise. That will do. We really don't want to hurt you. No percentages in that."

"Whatever. Zeke?"

Zeke slid along the ship to the locker and cached the rifle inside, then closed it and trooped back. As soon as he was a distance away, a figure emerged from the far airlock with a compressed-air-powered messenger rifle. His shot was quite wild, pinging on the hull almost twenty meters away. Apparently, pirates were lousy at regular space actions. Jake cursed and did a diving run, flipping over in mid-air and landing next to it with a thud. He hooked the loop at the end and carried it back to the bollards. Jake looped it over and engaged the locking lever. They were designed for quick release, and if not, then breakaway. Jake could throw the lever under tension to release the line, or if there was too much tension, the thin metal below would split, saving the ship's hull.

Jake keyed his radio. "Done. Attach the transfer line."

Jake waited while the figure on the far end attempted to attach a transfer line to the messenger line. He kept botching it. The transfer line needed both ends to be attached to the messenger, then Jake would haul the messenger in and attach the transfer line around a pully. Then whatever was attached to the two loose ends of the line made a loop that could be wheeled back and forth between the ships.

Jake waited a good five minutes, but the figure on the other side kept screwing up. Now he appeared to have tangled the whole line together. This was going to take forever.

He went on the radio. "Do you need assistance?" Jake asked. "I can do this much faster than you can. Clip your end to your hull, and I'll pull the slack over and attach the messenger here. Then you can pull it over."

"Stay put, Petrel, otherwise you'll get a laser in the face," the woman's voice said. Where had he heard that voice?

"What's the problem?" Nadine asked.

"I've never done this before. It's hard," Demitrios said.

"Tying a rope is hard?"

"It's not a rope, it's a line. These bollards or bollocks or whatever they are have to feed a certain way. And it's metal, so it doesn't bend the right way."

"How difficult can it be?"

"Do you want to come back and do it?"

"Not really. D, we need this to get the goods."

"I know. We need a plan B."

"Do you want to go and get them?"

"I can't maneuver a hundred kilograms by myself, even in zero-G. I'll crash. I'm no good at zero-G maneuvers."

"Why the hell did we bring you then?"

"To hit and shoot people, not tie knots. Give me somebody to hit. I'll do that. Right now, I really want to hit somebody."

"Pirate ship, this is Third Officer Vidal. I'm the deck officer. We really want this to be over and done with, so how about we just load up your goods, and jet them over from the airlock."

"We're not a pirate ship."

"Of course. What is your ship name?"

"Previous Solution."

"Okay, Previous Solution, do you want your ransom or not?"

Jake stood, listening. This was on the ship-to-ship channel. Both sides heard this. Why was Vidal intervening?

"Fine, that's a good idea. Let our guy get inside our lock, and you can send it over."

"We have people ready to go."

"Just one. Send Jake over with the goods. The others stay."

"He'll have to make multiple trips."

"That's fine."

"Very well. Jake, LaFleur, back to the airlock. Jake will pick up two boxes and jet them over, then come back for the other two."

Jake and Zeke returned into the airlock and popped their helmets open as the door closed.

"Listen up, everybody," Vidal said. "New plan. Jake, this first box has mixed platinum and others. Jet it across and give it to their guy. This second box has a sand caster round. While he's looking at the first one, pop it open and the round will fire five seconds later. We've reduced it to about a quarter charge, but it will still bang around."

He paused and looked at Suzanne. "Suzanne figures she can hit the laser control lines with a rifle from here. As soon as the charge goes off and Suzanne takes out the laser, LaFleur and I will jet across," he said, indicating

Zeke. "We'll both be armed with shotguns and revolvers. Any questions?"

"They'll shoot me in the airlock once the charge goes off," Jake said.

"While that wouldn't be much of a waste, I don't think they will. One of their guys obviously doesn't know what he's doing. And if they had more help, they wouldn't have agreed to us bringing the goods over ourselves, so they must be a small crew. The one idiot in the lock will be stunned by the charge. Then LaFleur and I will be there with the shotguns before you can say 'Imperial proclamation.' We'll take control of their ship, get back our PMGs, and be done with this idiotic affair."

"This will never work," Jake said.

"Of course it will. Speed and surprise always overcomes an unprepared enemy."

"They were pretty prepared when they got the drop on us," Jake said.

"Special circumstances," Vidal replied and glared at Jake. "Everybody ready? Good." Vidal didn't wait for an answer.

Vidal sealed his helmet and everybody hurried to do the same. Then they stepped out of sight while Jake stepped up to the airlock. When the door light turned blue, he swung the outer door open and stepped out with the first two cases.

"He's coming over now with the first two boxes," Jake heard Vidal say over the comm.

Jake steadied himself, activated his suit jets, and began to slowly cross between the ships. He couldn't go too fast. Items might not have weight in space, but they did have mass, and speeding up and slowing down cost fuel.

Jake floated toward the cargo lock. He could see a person inside it. "Coming in with the goods," Jake said over the comm. He slipped through the cargo lock and stopped himself using a toe bar. A huge figure in an oversized hard suit stood in front of him, holding an odd-looking rifle.

"That's a gauss rifle," Jake said.

"Relax," said the man in front of him. "I won't shoot you if you've followed instructions. Open the cases."

He hadn't seen a gauss rifle since he'd had to kill his former best friend, who had turned out to be a weapons smuggler and had framed him for murder.

Jake struggled to focus. He opened the first case and slid it across the airlock floor. The man glanced down, and Jake popped the second one open and shoved it across the floor. He made sure the shove propelled him backward so that he floated out of the airlock.

Jake grabbed another bar and swung himself out to the side. Facing away from the Previous Solution, he had a clear view of Vidal and Zeke launching themselves across space toward him just as the hatchway vomited a huge plume of sand. He saw flashes coming from the airlock as Suzanne began shooting at the laser. Two. Three. Four. She stopped. Jake saw his aspect change in regards to the Petrel. The maneuvering jets must be firing, he thought, as the Previous Solution spun over. He looked back to the ship's stern to see if he could see the blue glow that meant the fusion engine was engaging.

He had a perfect view as the Previous Solution's engine vanes exploded.

***

"Idiot," screamed Captain Marchello. "I told you to hit the other ship."

"But captain, we haven't fired the mass driver this trip. I told you we needed to calibrate."

"Silence! Silence! You dare to speak back to me." The captain began to slap the gunner's face with his white uniform gloves. The captain always carried the gloves with him, but rarely wore them.

173

"We were to hit the TGI pirate. Now we have injured that innocent Free Trader." The captain slapped the gunner again.

The first officer cleared his throat. It had been bad luck for everybody. Bad luck that the captain was on the bridge when they detected the two ships. Bad luck that those ships had not detected the Bountiful Onion before it got within shooting distance. Didn't either of those ships have anybody on sensor watch? Of course, it might have something to do with all the sand floating around. And, bad luck that they had never fired the mass driver before, so of course it was not firing true.

"Captain, there is some question as to who the attacker was and who was attacked."

"Nonsense. You clearly saw the TGI ship sending a boarding party to capture that poor trader."

"Er, yes, but there was damage on both sides. More on the TGI ship, it looks like. Perhaps, sir, it would be best to send two boarding parties to secure and sail both ships. We can take them both back to lower orbit for adjudication. Them and their cargo."

"Why would I want to do that? We will just let the trader go."

"I believe that this is the trader that was purchasing at the restricted colonies. We should look into that, and its cargo might be of interest. It might be necessary to secure their cargo here, on board, for safety's sake. We could recompense them, of course, with GG credits."

Meaning an opportunity for the ship to pay discounted company currency for real platinum, thought the first officer.

The captain paced and looked thoughtful for several moments. "An excellent idea, number one, excellent." The first officer let out a sigh of relief. "We do need to ensure security and stability on the Rim. Prepare two boarding parties and occupy both ships. I'll be in my cabin." The captain strode out.

The first officer turned back to his crew. At least some things were going his way today. Now all he needed to do was find two boarding parties that wouldn't shoot themselves in the foot.

14

Jake did not enjoy being in jail, again.

It wasn't really jail but a four-person stateroom with four acceleration couches stacked on top of each other and a fresher in the back. He shared it with Zeke and two engineering crewmen from the Petrel that he knew slightly. They were both older, thin, sober men who talked little. They could have been brothers.

The Bountiful Onion had "arrested" both ships pending an investigation. That entailed sending large armed boarding parties onto both of them and collecting and handcuffing both crews. They were left handcuffed for several hours before they were moved on board the Body Odor, as Jake had overheard the crew call it. There was a cursory search for weapons before they were locked in the staterooms and then called out for questioning. The two engineering crewmen went first.

"Just you and me, Jake," Zeke said.

"I guess so. Did you see what happened?"

"No, but I talked to one of the bridge guys. That other ship fired on the Previous Solution."

"Why did they do that?"

"Nobody knows."

"And why are we locked up?"

"Nobody knows that either."

"Huh."

"Jake, a question."

"Yes?"

"How did the Previous Solution lady know your name?"

"What are you talking about?"

"She called you by name on the radio channel. How do you know her?"

"I don't know her. I never saw her. But . . . her voice did sound familiar."

"How so?"

"Like somebody I knew at the academy."

"Somebody you knew at the Merchant's Academy is a pirate?"

"I don't know. Why are you asking?"

"Jake, she knew your name, and we never used your name over the comms. Plus, how did they find us and sneak up on us? Space is big."

"Space is big, but we were broadcasting a huge pile of messages. That's why we were running without the engines on. We used the whole fusion plant output for the antennas to send messages. They probably heard that."

"Still, it is suspicious."

Jake stayed in his room for almost two days before he was called in for questioning. He was chained hand and foot and escorted to a room where he sat in front of a very tired-looking man with first officer's bars and a well-dressed man with a pair of white gloves that looked like silk and captain's bars seemingly tattooed on his suit.

"Jake Stewart?" the first officer asked.

"Yes sir."

"You are an 'indentured voluntary Militia' TGI auxiliary specialist level 0."

"Yes sir."

"Why were you boarding that other ship?"

"They shot at us."

"You admit you were trying to capture it?"

"No sir. They shot at us and disabled us, and then used their weapons to hold us hostage. They demanded a ransom. My job was to bring the ransom over to the Previous Solution."

"And you blew a scuttling charge in their airlock?"

"Uh, no, sir. We exploded a sand caster round in the airlock."

"Exploded a sand caster round in the airlock? What was the point of that?"

"Cover, while we shot out their laser gun, sir."

"How would you shoot it out? You said you had no functioning weapons."

"One of our crew had a rifle, sir."

The captain laughed.

"You expect me to believe that you were caught by surprise, and your ship was damaged, and you expected to take the other ship's weapons out with a rifle—a hand-held firearm—and then blow a hole in them with a sand caster round."

"Uh, yes, sir."

"The Previous Solution says they were maneuvering to render assistance to you when you shot at them, disabled their laser, threatened them, sent out a boarding party, and blew a hole in the airlock with a breaching charge," the captain said.

"The sensor logs should support our version, sir?"

"Your sensor logs stop abruptly before the battle starts."

"Would that be when they shot us, sir?"

"Or you turned them off. We know who the pirate here is and who is not."

The first officer cleared his throat. "Captain, there is some dispute here, sir. Some of the sensor logs are

178

ambiguous."

"Enough, First. I know a pirate when I see one, and I see one right here in front of me. That poor young lady, she must have been terrified to see these TGI thugs attacking her ship."

Jake looked at the captain. "Poor young lady? Umm, was this young lady about my age, blonde, athletic build, a little shorter than me, captain?"

"Aha. You even know who you were attacking. You must have been stalking her."

Jake's heart sank. He knew that "young lady." It was Nadine. She worked for somebody else, somebody who didn't like TGI. She was very good at lying and had managed to get him framed for murder during his last semester at school. And now it seemed she was framing him as a pirate.

"We're not thugs, sir. We're TGI staff and we were just defending ourselves."

"So you say. Why did you have extra crew with no duties who were not on your books?"

"Sir?"

"You are three people over complement, and none of you have any shipboard ratings. But you are all trained in weapons. You are not, technically, crew. You must be shock troops, paid hooligans, to terrorize the crews you capture."

The first officer stirred, and Jake could see him mouthing "hooligans," shaking his head, and then speaking up. "Captain, these stories do not make sense, and I do not think that more questioning will make any difference. We should just lock them back in their rooms, finish repairs, and continue back to the inner Belt."

The captain nodded. "That is an excellent suggestion, First. I agree."

"You do, sir? I mean, thank you, sir." The first officer looked very surprised.

"Yes, an excellent plan. We will incarcerate the crews

from both ships on board the Bountiful Onion and put our own crews on their ships to bring them back to the inner rim where we will arbitrate this with TGI."

"Very well, sir. I will make the arrangements." The first officer stood up.

"But that is not all. We will incarcerate the crews of the ships, but this one, and the two others, the boarders, they are not technically crew, are they?"

"Well, they are not on the books as such, no, sir."

"Then they are hooligans. Pirates. Do you know the penalty for piracy, young hooligan?"

"Incarceration?" Jake guessed. He wanted to try out how the word sounded.

"Hah. No. Death. Out the airlock with all three of you."

***

The first officer could be heard protesting as a crewman brought Jake out of the office. They hustled him down the corridor and down a deck to his jail stateroom. They unlocked Jake and pushed him through the door. Zeke looked up. "What happened to you? What did they say?"

"They said I was sentenced to death for piracy, and that I was to be put out the airlock. Oh, and you and Suzanne too."

"That's funny, Jake. What did they actually say?"

"That was it. They think we attacked the PS and were boarding it to steal it."

"You can't be serious."

"They were arguing when I left. I'm not sure if it's real or if they were just trying to mess with me."

"Suzanne wasn't even in the boarding party. Why is she being labeled a pirate and not Vidal?"

"They checked the records. We're not listed as regular crew so their captain thinks we're pirates."

"Oh."

Jake flicked the door switch. It was locked, of course.

"So, Zeke, your career as a TGI employee reaches an ignominious end."

"I do not know that word."

"Ignominious? Um, famous, but famous for bad things."

"I do like the sound of that. Perhaps I will be remembered as Zeke the ignominious."

"Zeke, you know we are in jail, and they are going to space us. Let's focus on that."

Zeke gave his Francais shrug. "I don't usually worry about those things, Jake. Something will come up. Besides, it has been fun so far."

"Fun?"

"I've gone to space. I've jumped between spaceships. I've been on other stations. And I have made a good friend. You, Jake." He clapped Jake on the shoulder. "Has it not been fun for you as well, my friend?"

"No. It's been difficult. Tiring. Embarrassing. Humiliating."

"What was humiliating?"

"Getting arrested. Getting sent to jail."

"But some of it must have been fun?"

"That's me, Zeke." Jake sat down on one of the couches and put his head in his hands. "I'm not much for fun, really."

Zeke smiled. "Jake, Suzanne and I thought you were too serious when we met you."

"Too serious?"

"Oh, we liked you, but you were strange. You took everything so seriously. You studied things. You made notes. You tried so hard. It was difficult not to giggle when you kept missing the target."

Jake raised his eyebrows. "I didn't think it was funny."

"We know. Suzanne and I talked about it. You were trying too hard. If you had been more relaxed, it would have been better. But you do not relax very well."

"No, I don't. But it's good to be prepared."

"You should relax. All your preparation and here you are, locked in a room about to die by being thrown out airlock for being a pirate. How did your preparation help you there?"

"Not very much."

"You see? But for me, I like to try new things. I do not want to die, but I do not want to not do something because I am afraid. And I want to have fun while I am alive. This has been very frightening, this Militia ship, but very rewarding."

"It's not a Militia ship, Zeke."

"As you say."

"And we should have been prepared for something like this. There are pirates all over and we weren't exactly subtle about what we were buying up or how much. I should have known someone was going to decide it was worth it to try and hijack us. I should have planned for this scenario."

"Yes. That is what Suzanne said when she spoke of you. She said you overprepared."

"Suzanne spoke about me? What did she say?"

Zeke smiled. "Why, are you interested in what she said?"

Jake sputtered a bit, and Zeke smiled again. "I am sorry, Jake. I cannot resist teasing. You know she talks about you. She likes you."

"She likes Vidal more."

"She did. He was a challenge. Suzanne likes challenges. You were not so challenging."

"She was just stringing me along."

"Just a little bit. But she did say you were very nice." Zeke coughed. "Don't worry, Jake. You will think of something to keep us both from being thrown out the airlock. You always do. And if not, at least rabbits will not pee on my grave," Zeke said. He walked over to one of the other couches and lounged back on it, staring at the ceiling.

One of the other men began to cough. "What's wrong with him?" Jake asked as he walked over to him.

"I do not know. But he has been sleeping and coughing all day."

"What is that rash on his face?" Jake asked.

Zeke shrugged. "I am not a doctor. You must be a sound sleeper. He and the other one coughed all night. You slept through it."

Jake stepped back a little. The man didn't look well.

There was a bong and the door opened. A crewman with a shotgun stood behind the rating who had brought them there.

"Captain says you go out the airlock in twenty-four hours. He wants to know what you want for your last meal."

Jake awoke after a long and surprisingly restful sleep. He felt clearheaded, focused, and with a number of arguments against spacing him foremost in his mind. Somebody in his reading had said the possibility of being hanged in the morning concentrates the mind wonderfully. Boy, were they right. He was ready to argue.

Jake got up to use the fresher. The cabin stank. A lot. Jake hadn't smelt a cabin that bad since he had been working on tramp freighters, and the workers had crapped in their suits during a long shift. Somebody had done the same here.

He flicked the cabin light on. Neither of the techs moved. Jake looked more closely. Their faces were completely covered with a rash. Their breathing was more like wheezing, and were drenched in sweat.

"Zeke. Wake up." Jake walked over to shake Zeke awake and stopped himself. Zeke looked flushed and his breathing was shallow. There was a slight rash blooming on his face.

"Oh, shit," Jake said out loud. He'd never seen this but he'd heard about it. His mother had said it had happened when he was very young, too young to remember. A ship had come in and brought a disease. First, people came down with a fever and cough, and then a rash. Something like 70 percent of them had died within a few days. What was it she had called it? Jake racked his memory. Oh, yeah.

Measles.

Jake raced over to the door and started banging on it. He was scared of measles. He pushed the comm and yelled into it. No one answered. He went to the head and soaked a towel in cool water, then placed it on Zeke's head. He was burning to the touch.

Jake paced back and forth. He didn't feel sick. No cough. No sweating. He must have been inoculated. That's right—after the outbreak when he was a kid, everyone got inoculated. But he didn't think that was common. It certainly didn't look like Zeke or the other crewmen had been.

What about the rest of the crew? Suzanne? He banged on the door and screamed some more. Still no answer. What about the crew of the Bountiful Onion? If they hadn't been inoculated, Jake wondered how many of them had gotten sick. Was anybody even out there?

"You are immune?" Suzanne asked as the door closed behind the men carrying Sue's corpse away.

"Well, I've had my shots," Nadine said.

"What are shots?"

"Immunizations. Didn't they stick a needle in you when you joined the Militia?"

"No, what for?"

"To keep you from getting sick. Or making other people sick. All the Militia get them."

"We were not put in the Militia in the regular way. We did not get any shots. What about Sue?"

"She wasn't part of my regular company. I guess she

184

wasn't immunized." Nadine shrugged. "I never asked. What does it matter for you, though? If you don't get sick, you'll just get thrown out the airlock with the other pirates." Nadine giggled a little to herself.

"Jake won't let that happen. He is too clever. He will get us out," Suzanne said.

"Jake won't let it happen?" Now Nadine struggled not to laugh out loud. "How? Will he attack them all and kill them with his bare hands?"

"Of course not. He will have read the 'Official Rules Regarding Space Executions' or whatever the appropriate rulebook is called, and he will have found a clause that only allows them to execute people if they have a pink spaceship, and since this spaceship is blue they cannot execute anybody until they paint it pink, and then he will show them that there is a shortage of pink paint, so we will be safe. He is very good with rulebooks. This is why he is here."

"That sounds like Jake."

"How do you know Jake? You knew his name before we told you. You have met him before?"

"You could say that."

"Where did you meet him?"

"Oh, around. Who shot our laser out?"

"That was me," Suzanne said.

"Good shooting. Where did you learn that?"

"Around." They both laughed.

"Do you have any other useful skills?" Nadine asked. "Spaceship skills, perhaps?"

"I do. Where did you get your ship from?"

Nadine poured a cup of water. "Well, that's a funny story."

Zeke and the techs got sicker. Jake ignored the techs— he didn't know them, and they weren't his friends. Zeke was lucid for a while during the night and Jake tried to talk with him and keep him calm.

"I am going to die," Zeke said.

"Not necessarily."

"How many people die?"

"I'm not sure."

"You are not a very good liar, Jake. I am sure you know these things. You must have read about it in one of your books. How many sick people die?"

Jake sat back and looked at Zeke. "A lot. A third, half, three-quarters. I'm not sure, but a lot."

"That is not good."

"Nope." Jake looked away.

"But you, you are not sick?"

"No. Something like this came through when I was a kid. I think I must have been immunized."

"I feel very hot. Can you get me some water, please, Jake?"

Jake got a cup and ran water from the tap. Zeke sucked it down, then started to cough. Jake lifted Zeke up, trying to help him breathe.

"I don't really want to die, Jake," Zeke said as the coughing abated. "I have so much to do. There is so much fun still to be had."

"You won't die. You'll pull through. You'll see. You'll survive long enough to get thrown out the airlock with me," Jake joked. He thought he caught a small smile cross Zeke's lips as his friend closed his eyes.

"Thank you, Jake. You are a good friend."

"You're welcome," Jake said, trying not to let the tears get the better of him. "You have been a good friend too. I've had fun. I mean, it's been difficult. Tiring. Embarrassing. Humiliating. But sometimes fun."

Jake watched his best friend fall asleep, possibly for the last time. Jake watched for a long time before he was sure Zeke was still breathing. The room was hot, and it stank. He was thirsty, tired, and probably dying.

And when he died, Suzanne would say, "Good old

Jake. He was very nice."

Zeke didn't wake up the next morning. He was still breathing, but it was very shallow. Jake tried to give him some water, but he mostly choked on it. Using his fingers and a spoon he eventually got the door controls off the wall, but the door was mechanically locked from outside, so he couldn't bypass the lock.

When Jake checked on the techs in the evening, one had died. The other died soon after. Zeke still wouldn't take water.

The next morning, the door opened and three crewmen in locked softsuits stood outside. One had a shotgun pointed at Jake.

"Into the head. Narin, check them out."

Jake retreated into the bathroom, hands held high.

They checked the two techs and dragged them out into the hall without a word. Then they checked Zeke for a pulse.

"This one's still alive."

"Leave him there. No room in the infirmary." The men began to walk out of the room.

"Wait," Jake said. "You have to help him," But the men just backed out and locked them in.

Jake sat with Zeke for the next twenty-four hours. Jake had access to a full selection of RGB trays with a microwave slot, so he had plenty to eat and drink. He tried to feed Zeke, but Zeke could barely swallow water. The techs' beds stank. Jake tried to clean the couches where they had defecated with water from the tap, but it did little to help the smell.

It was a long night. The power fluctuated twice, and Jake heard a collision alarm sound for a full ten minutes before it turned off. An hour before normal breakfast time he felt the ship fire thrusters with no warning. The comms didn't work, or no one was answering, and the door remained locked. Jake had no idea what was going on.

But by mid-day Zeke was somewhat better. Weak, but his fever had lessened and he could swallow without choking. He'd fouled himself as well, so Jake dragged him into the shower and helped him hose himself down. They had water rations for four people on the meter, so Jake made the most of it.

They sat there all day. Jake began to sweat. He was getting sick.

Zeke woke up in the afternoon. "Thank you for taking care of me, Jake."

"Don't worry about it. You'll be able to return the favor. I'm getting sick."

"Are you sure? I thought you were immunized."

"I'm sweating. I must be getting sick. That's the first symptom, right?"

"No, coughing and runny eyes. That's what I had."

"Huh, different people get different symptoms, I guess."

"It's not a symptom. It's just hot in here."

"What?"

"We're just heating up. It must be forty degrees Celsius in here."

"That doesn't sound right."

Jake thought about this. He was hot, but he hadn't begun coughing and he didn't feel weak. "Uh oh." Jake walked over to the air vent and stuck his hand next to it. There was no airflow. He put his ear to it for a moment. "No sounds, no air. The vents are closed. Somebody sealed the different parts of the ship off from each other."

"Why are we not dead of asphyxiation?" Suzanne asked, fanning herself. She had stripped down to her underwear and was still sweating.

"It's a big ship. They sealed the different decks from each other, but there is still air circulating around. Normally you don't die from lack of oxygen but rather an excess of carbon monoxide. But if there aren't a lot of people here, then we won't breathe out much. We can live for a long time in this big a deck, particularly if there are only a few of us," Nadine said. She was also nearly nude and still sweating.

"But why the heat?"

"They turned off the air circulation, and there are all sorts of electrical equipment, microwaves, comm units, computers, and people. We all produce heat and there's nowhere for it to go."

"Then we will bake to death?"

"Not quickly. Some of the heat will radiate out to space. What's that?"

There was a clacking sound outside the door.

Nadine and Suzanne jumped up and stood in front of the door. It slowly ground open, revealing a very thin, very pale-faced man staring at them. He stopped when he realized he was facing two sweaty girls in their underwear.

Nadine smiled at him. "You're here! Thank god. We were so worried." She leaned forward and kissed him on the lips, pulling his head toward her.

He stepped back, confused.

"Mmmph. Oh, baby, are you as hot as I am?" Nadine said. She put one foot behind his leg, then leaned down forward and pushed.

The man tripped over her foot and hit his head—bump—on the floor. His eyes closed.

Nadine smiled. "Hormones. Gets them every time." She grabbed the man and began to drag him into the cabin. "Get some clothes on, and we'll go get your brother and rulebook boy and get out of here."

15

Jake and Zeke were sitting playing cards with a pack they had found in one of the engineering techs' bag when the door opened. Suzanne stood there.

"Zeke! Jake! Are you okay?"

"Yes. I was sick, but I'm much better. Jake got me through. What about you?" Zeke asked as he got up and embraced his sister.

"Nadine and I did not get sick," Suzanne said. "I guess we were lucky."

Nadine walked in behind Suzanne and flashed a smile at Zeke, then she winked at Jake.

"Hello, Nadine," Jake said.

"Hello, Jakey boy."

"You two know each other?" Zeke asked.

"Oh, we've met. She shot me, kidnapped me with her starship, chained me to a bunk, and made me help her steal a cache of old-empire weapons."

Nadine smiled at Zeke. "And that was just our first date. It gets even better after that."

"Brother, Nadine has offered me a job," Suzanne said, turning back to Zeke.

"Doing what?" Zeke said.

"Being a pirate. Sorry, being a corporate operative," she said, nodding to Nadine.

Nadine shrugged. "They are very similar. It's kind of a situational difference, really. Your sister said she burned down a bar. That sounds like the kind of person I need working with me. She also said that you beat up a guy so that you would get arrested and put in the Militia, and that you like to do exciting things. If that's true, I might be able to offer you employment as well. That is, provided we get off this disease-infested hellhole."

"And how do you propose we do that?" Jake asked.

"It's simple. The captain told me that he had 'arrested' both of our ships, and put the crews on the Onion. He also arrested all of our PGMs. He didn't have enough trained crew to pilot the two captured ships, so he was going to tow them alongside. There are two other ships out there. Probably no measles-ridden corpses on them, either."

"How can you know that?"

"Well, thinking back, Sue was coughing and sweating before we ever got caught by the Onion. So, I think she brought it on board, not you. I say we get my ship and fly our butts as far away as possible," Nadine said. "But first, we're going to get my PMGs."

"What about the crew on board the Bountiful Onion?" Jake said. "We need to get these people to a station before they all die."

"Jake, not to put too fine a point on it, but unless you are a doctor with a bunch of pills or something, the ones who are sickest will all die anyway. At least, the ones who aren't already dead. And besides, forty-eight hours ago they promised to heave you out an airlock without a suit."

"You convinced the captain I was a pirate."

"I may have embellished it a bit, but I figured he'd just lock you up and let me go. I didn't think he'd order you dead."

"Nadine, we can't just let everybody die. We need to

see if anybody needs help."

"You first, Jakey," Nadine said.

"Fine," Jake said. He shoved his way past Nadine and marched out into the hallway. He began searching the corridors and other rooms. Nadine followed, arguing. Suzanne helped support Zeke as they followed close behind. They found eight corpses in four different cabins just in the first corridor.

Vidal was the second one.

"Well, shit," Jake said.

"Friend of yours?" Nadine asked.

"He was our boss. He was an ass. Wanted to space me."

"Why didn't you kill him first?"

"What?"

"If he was going to kill you, why not get him first?"

"I don't do that, Nadine."

"I know. Big character flaw on your part, Jakey. Say, do you like that girl?" Nadine nodded her head to the corridor where Suzanne was sitting with Zeke as he rested.

"What?"

"Suzanne. She kind of likes you, but she thinks you're a bit boring."

"Boring?"

"Anytime I talk to you for a long period of time, Jake, you end up just repeating what I say."

"Thanks."

"Are you sorry he's dead?" Nadine said, indicating Vidal's body in front of them.

Jake looked at Vidal's body. He thought a long time before saying anything.

"A little. But he would have killed me, I think, if he could have gotten away with it."

"Well, that's progress of a sort, I guess. You still should have killed him, Jake."

"You know I couldn't do that."

Jake stepped out to break the news to Suzanne. She

took it well, considering how close Jake thought they had become during their time on the Petrel.

They kept searching the cabins, looking for somebody alive. None of the cabins were locked and they all had working comms, but they couldn't get anyone to answer on board and they couldn't get a line out to the other two ships.

They found the rest of Nadine's crew, Big D, in one of the cabins. He lay on his back, eyes open and staring at the ceiling.

"Poor bastard," Nadine said. "He once told me he was planning on getting killed in a shootout in a bar over a girl."

"A shootout over a girl?"

"Ideally two girls, he said." Nadine stepped forward and carefully closed his eyes. "Free trades, Big D. You weren't very smart, but you were useful." She sighed. "What an epitaph, huh, Jake? Not very smart, but useful."

"I guess mine would be 'Nice, but boring,'" Jake said.

"Ha! That's true," Nadine said. "Wow, who would have thought you could crack a joke at a time like this. You should work on that, Jake."

They tried to climb to the deck above, but the hatch wouldn't open. The mechanism appeared to be jammed. They turned and tried to go back down the ship and were able to make it into the cargo decks and the connector tunnel before the lights went out. The emergency power came on.

"This is not good," Jake said.

"No, it's not," Nadine said.

They climbed back up to the cargo deck, collected the others, and found a working computer with access to the ship's logs.

"There are a number of general notices on the ship's bulletin board," Jake said as he typed into the system. "The first officer has sent several. He says it's definitely measles. Crewmen who do not have 'Inoculation 73' will probably catch it. They were shaping course for the Roundhouse station at best acceleration—.5 G—for medical assistance."

"That's good news."

"That lasted for two more shifts. The first officer seemed in control of the situation."

"That's good. Then what?" Nadine said, looking over Jake's shoulder.

"Then he's dead. And a bunch of others."

"Crap."

"The captain took over. He cut power to everywhere except the bridge and engineering and ordered each section of the ship to isolate themselves from the others."

"That's what happened last night. That is why it was so hot," Suzanne said. Zeke was sitting with his back against a wall next to her. He looked pale still, but better than he'd looked a day ago.

"He also cut off external communication for some reason," Jake continued. "Without it, we can't call anyone else."

"What an idiot," Nadine said.

"He's afraid of getting sick, I think. He sent out an emergency transmission, though. But . . . looks like he sent it in the wrong direction. No one is going to receive that message for a long time."

"Why is the power out now?" Zeke asked. "And where are the rest of the crew? Are they all dead?"

"I don't know. Circuit breaker blew, maybe? There's nothing here," Jake said. "There's no more posts after that."

"How are the computers working, then?" Suzanne said.

"Different circuit. They are tied into the bridge."

"Well, at least it is not as hot as before," Suzanne said.

Jake and Nadine looked at each other.

"What?" Suzanne asked.

"That's bad," Jake said. "Each deck has heaters. That's what was keeping all of us warm. Them and all the electrical equipment, pumps, screens, stuff like that on each deck. But with the power to the deck shut off, we're cooling down."

"How cold will it get?" Suzanne asked.

"Two hundred degrees below zero, maybe?"

"What should we do, then?"

"Well, we cannot stay here," Zeke said. "I do not want to survive measles only to freeze to death. We need to go somewhere. We need a ship."

"Mine has a great autopilot, and we can get out of here in a hurry," Nadine said.

"You're forgetting that your engines got shot to pieces," Jake said.

"Just the nozzles."

"Can't steer without them. They direct the particle stream."

"Spoilsport. You can fix them."

"No I can't, and even if I could, it will take time. Lots of time. We should take the Petrel. It's bigger. More fuel capacity."

"Takes a bigger crew to run. There are only four of us. Can you pilot it?"

"Not really," Jake admitted. "But you can."

"Maybe. What's in it for me?"

"Not dying?"

"It's you they are going to space, buddy. I'm just along for the ride, and I'm willing to get off this death ship, but really, why do I need to leave? Far as I can tell, I'm immune to this disease. I could just stay here and wait till everybody gets better. Or somebody, or nobody. Then take my complaint about being pirated by a TGI ship coreward."

"Nobody will believe you. And if they do check the records, they'll find out you fired first."

"Could be. But maybe they won't. Either way, I don't get spaced."

"Jake, come over here, please," Suzanne called. She was

looking at a different screen.

"Yes, what?"

"I found a navigation screen. What does this mean, this red thing here on our course vector?"

"That's the collision notification. It says . . . it says we're gonna hit something if we continue on this course."

"Is that not bad?"

"Yes, but we won't hit for another two hours. We'll worry about that in a minute. Nadine."

Nadine folded her arms across her chest. "What?"

"If Zeke, Suzanne, and I stay, when everyone gets better, they'll space us. We need to get away from here, far enough away that we can send a message for help and not get caught. The Petrel is our best bet. I can fix the broken control runs on the Petrel, but I can't fix the busted drive nozzle on your ship."

"So?"

"You can take a chance on freezing if you want, but we're taking our ship and going. We need to get somewhere to send help for everyone on this ship. If anyone's still alive, we need to try and help them. The Petrel is the best way to do that. If you pilot us away from here, we'll drop you off somewhere safe."

"You'd trust me to do that?"

"Nope. But I can navigate. I'll know where you're driving us."

"Excuse me," said Zeke, "but I have a question about this collusion thing. We will hit something, correct?"

"Collision. Yes, but not for hours, and we'll just steer around it," Nadine said.

"But we have no power, which means no engines, correct? How will we steer around it? And who will steer around it? You say most of the crew are dead. And how will we engage the steering? Who is on the bridge to issue the commands?"

"Crap," Nadine and Jake said together.

It took ten minutes to find the emergency access tunnel, and another thirty minutes to crawl down the tunnel to the engineering section, where the backup engine controls would be. They needed to open three different hatches but the central computer had locked them all shut when the captain disconnected the sections. Jake had to pry the control panels off and open them by hand. Finally, they made it to the last hatch in front of engineering.

"Tell me again why we are doing this?" Zeke asked.

"Because Jakey doesn't want all these sick people to die. We'll fire the engines and put them in a stable orbit."

"Then we'll get to the Petrel and move where we can contact someone to come and rescue them," Jake said.

Nadine glared at him. "I still think we should take my ship. Bah. This door is stuck too."

"Will there still be power to run the engines when we get inside?" Zeke asked.

"Yes, nobody ever shuts down a fusion plant," Jake said.

"Why not?"

"Can't restart them. Only the Old Empire could restart a failed fusion plant."

Jake pried open the control panel. He held two wires in his teeth and began typing on the diagnostic unit Nadine had produced. Jake was surprised at her—it was manufactured by Fluke, a very reputable firm. She hadn't seemed the type to spend money on good testing equipment. "There. In we go."

Nadine swung the hatch open and walked inside. Jake followed.

There was a loud bang, and Nadine dropped.

"What? What?" Jake said. Zeke pushed him down behind some equipment. Suzanne reached out and grabbed Nadine and pulled her in behind with them.

"Who are you?" a voice yelled. "What do you want?"

"Who are you?" Jake countered. He couldn't see who

was speaking. They must have been hiding around the corner. "And why are the engines off? We're going to impact an asteroid."

"An asteroid?"

"Turn the engines back on. We need some thrust."

Nadine was rolling around in agony, on the floor. Zeke and Suzanne grabbed her and held her tight.

"You're the pirates, aren't you?" the voice said.

"We're not pirates."

"Why aren't you dead? From the plague?"

"Some of us are. And the rest will be soon if we don't change course!"

"You lie. I will call the captain. If you move, I will shoot you."

Jake looked at Zeke. "He can't shoot us while we stay here."

"Is that the engine core? I have never been in an engine room. It is very large," Zeke said.

"Nadine, are you okay?" Jake asked.

"No, I'm not okay, asshole. My arm is broken."

Suzanne was working on her arm. "She is correct. It is broken. But it is a clean break. The bullet was a ship load, but it hit straight on. We will have to splint her."

"You broke our friend's arm," Jake yelled.

"I will shoot you if you come closer."

"Jake, he won't," whispered Suzanne.

"What do you mean?"

"He's out of ammo. I should have heard the clack as he broke it open and reloaded. He had only the one shot. Zeke, you heard it too, yes? He fired his only shot."

"Yes, Jake. Suzanne is right. Let's charge him."

"Wait, are you sure?" Jake asked.

"Of course. Don't you remember Sergeant Russell's discussion about listening and counting rounds?"

"No. I thought it was boring."

"Jake, there are three of us. Even if he has more ammo, if we rush him he will not be able to shoot all three of us."

"I don't think I like those odds," Jake said.

Nadine moaned again as Suzanne tried to hold her arm steady.

"What if it's a whatchacallit, automatic shotgun?" Jake said.

"It wasn't. Didn't you see it when they boarded? They don't have auto-shot guns."

"They don't?" Jake strove to remember. He had seen the guns, but he couldn't tell one gun from another. "But how do we tell?" Jake asked.

"Jake, sometimes you must just take the risk, yes? Jump before thinking," Zeke said. "Sometimes there just is no time to plan. You tell me we need to start the engines. This is how to do it."

"Okay, fine. You're right." Jake turned to Suzanne. She was propping Nadine up against the wall. Nadine was cradling her arm. "We go on three. Ready? One, two . . . wait."

"Three!" Suzanne and Zeke yelled and broke cover. Jake cursed and ran after them.

Suzanne was right. The crewman just sat there. The gun laid on the floor.

"No bullets?" she asked the crewman.

"No. I found it here. It had only the one."

"You broke our friend's arm," Jake said.

"What was I to do? You are pirates, and I'm so weak I can barely move." The man looked sweaty and feverish. He obviously wasn't well.

"What's your name?" Jake asked.

"Colau."

"Colau, we're going to crash into an asteroid if we don't get the engines on. And even if we don't hit anything, we're going to freeze to death soon after." Their breath was starting to fog in the air.

"Emperor's balls. What can we do?"

"Aren't you an engineer?"

"No. This is my first trip. I polished the floors and

cleaned."

"We need to get the engines on."

"But there is no fuel or reaction mass."

"What?"

"The captain. He made an error. He is not a very good captain, really. The deputy engineer said he dumped the fuel after the plague hit. I'm not sure why. I was very weak, and the deputy died soon after. They're all dead. It is just me down here."

"Okay. Plan B," Jake said. "Colau, you come with us."

"Where are we going?"

"Forward airlock, suit up, get over to the Petrel, fire it up, fix the control runs and get out of here. Colau, if you want to live, come with us."

It didn't take as long to go back as it did to go down the connection tube, but it still took time. Colau was weak and stumbled a lot. Jake helped him along. Zeke carried the empty shotgun, and Suzanne helped Nadine. They had foam-splinted her arm from an emergency med kit they had found in the engineering room and tied it across her chest. They'd also given her a pain shot.

"Whoo, that's good stuff," Nadine said. "Here we go, everyone. Race you!" With that, she started climbing one-handed up along the tube.

Soon they arrived in the upper cargo hold.

"Wait!" Nadine shouted and went to one of the cargo hold's doors. She began playing with the lock.

"Nadine, what the heck are you doing? We have no time," Jake said.

"We have at least forty-five minutes until we hit, and that's my platinum in there. They took it off my ship. And yours too. I know you were buying it. We'll just grab a couple hundred kilograms and go."

"You are pirates!" Colau said as he slumped to the floor against a wall.

"We don't have time. We'd need to spend an hour working on the lock and. . . ."

Zeke walked over to the far wall and collected a fire axe. He walked back, and with three swift two-handed swings, smashed the lock and the hasp right off the door.

"How about now, Jake?" Nadine said as the door swung open. "Do we have time now?"

"She could be a lot of fun," Zeke said, whispering to Jake.

"If you call getting shot fun," Jake said.

Despite Jake's protests, they all took as much as they could carry. Jake cursed but assisted by identifying the highest-value metals. If there was no talking them out of it, the least he could do was help speed up the process. They hauled cases up to the next-level airlock and dumped them in, then quickly suited up. Nadine was tethering cases to each of them as Jake looked out the airlock.

"Uh-oh," Jake said.

"Jake, what is it?" Zeke asked.

"They didn't link the ships right. You're supposed to attach towing lines, then you slave the boards, but it looks like the Petrel is just attached with towing lines," Jake said, turning back to the others.

Zeke and Suzanne looked confused but Nadine understood. "Jake means that towing lines aren't enough. They should have linked the computers so that both ships would fire their thrusters in tandem, otherwise the stresses could break the lines." She peered through the window next to Jake.

The Petrel was hanging behind the Bountiful Onion at the end of a single line. Two or three other lines had obviously broken and were lashing around. With only one point of attachment, the Petrel was free to move in all directions. It spun. It rolled. It wrapped around the tow line from time to time. Sometimes the tow line went slack and the Petrel drifted towards the Bountiful Onion. Anyone trying to board would have to be very careful. They would have to time their leap in three dimensions.

"That looks . . . difficult," Suzanne said.

"Okay, we'll just need to take it slow and easy. Hold on to the line. Go down hand over hand all the way—otherwise, you'll just bang into the ship and get crushed," Jake said.

"Jake, we cannot carry these cases and go hand over hand. We should jump instead," Zeke said. He might have still been a little weak, but he was still Zeke.

"We'll have to leave the goods behind. You'll get killed," Jake said.

"I'm not leaving a fortune in platinum here for Captain Onion or whoever he is," Nadine said.

"It's too dangerous."

"Of course it's dangerous, Jake!" Nadine said. "But sometimes you have to take a risk."

"That's the drugs talking," Jake said.

"Maybe. But I'm jumping."

"Jake." Suzanne stepped over and placed a hand on Jake's shoulder. "You are so good in zero-G, Jake. We will go first. You will make sure we are all safe. And it will be fun." She smiled at him. Jake sighed.

"Here, you and I can carry two of these cases," Nadine said, picking them up. "And the others only one. We will leave two behind. Hey, Zeke, Suzanne?"

"Yes?"

"Watch me. Just do what I do." She stepped forward and crouched.

"Wait," Jake said.

"Away we go! Whee!" Nadine, clutching two carrying cases of platinum to her chest, pushed off from the airlock and spun into space.

Jake cursed as he watched her spin over and over as she sailed toward the Petrel. But he needn't have worried, as she showed surprising grace. She extended her arms at just the right moment to control her spinning, executing a neat landing on the Petrel.

Wow, Jake thought. She's good. He didn't know much about Nadine's training, but it was apparent some of it had been in zero-G.

Suzanne stepped up to launch next, clutching two cases.

"Suzanne, wait, leave one of—"

She leaped out the airlock before Jake could protest. She kept close to the line. That was smart, Jake thought. She'd be able to grab it and slow if need be. She kept almost constant speed as she floated across. The Petrel spun beneath her, and Jake had an anxious moment when he thought she might have misjudged and would just miss the airlock. But she extended her arms out to slow her spin, and dragged a foot along the tow line to increase friction. She was almost there. Jake held his breath. He watched as she managed to land feet-first, but hard.

"Ow," Suzanne said over the comms. Jake let out a long breath. She'd made it and was waving back at them.

"Wow," Zeke said. "I'll go next."

"Zeke, no. You're not as practiced in zero-G and you're still weak and dizzy. Just pull yourself along the line until you get here. Don't take any cases."

"I will be fine, Jake. Do not worry." Zeke leaned down and grabbed two cases. Jake tried to snatch them back, but Zeke had already climbed away.

"Zeke, you don't have to do this. Just go slowly down the line hand over hand."

"And leave all the money? I shall not," he said. "And besides, if Nadine can do it and Suzanne can do it, I can also."

"Zeke, please. Don't try to show off," Jake said. "This isn't the time to be risky. You'll die."

"Everything will be fine. You worry too much, my friend," Zeke said, and he launched himself from the Bountiful Onion with a case in each hand.

"Zeke, wait!" Jake yelled.

Zeke had jumped too soon. He had jumped as the Petrel was rolling away from the Onion. He should have waited until it was rolling toward the Onion, then he would have hit the target as it was moving away from him—a gentle landing.

Instead, the Petrel reached the end of its attached line just as Zeke pushed off. At first Zeke seemed to be floating slowly toward the Petrel as it coasted to a stop, held by the tension in the tow line. The tow line was a braided metal cable, but even metal will stretch a bit. Just like a ball on a rubber band, the two-hundred-ton ship began to snap backwards toward the Onion. The Petrel began to race toward Zeke, gaining speed.

Zeke continued to coast, but his inexperience caused him to try to adjust the two cases he was carrying.

"Zeke, don't move your arms," Jake said into the channel. "You'll unbalance yourself."

"What?"

"You'll change your center of gravity and start to spin. Keep your arms steady."

But it was too late. Zeke began to roll and threw out one of his arms to steady himself, which induced a spin. Soon he was tumbling head over heels and side to side at the same time.

"Zeke, drop the cases. Drop the cases and try to stabilize yourself."

"I don't like this spin, Jake."

"Zeke. Drop the cases and try to get your roll under control. You need to land feet-first."

Zeke was now in an uncontrolled tumble. Worse, the Petrel was accelerating toward him, so he was going to hit hard. The towing cable was now slack and had bent in the middle.

"Zeke, watch out for the tow line."

Zeke plowed through the tow line. His foot caught on it as he spun by, pivoting him and sending him off-course, away from his landing zone. Now he was tumbling toward one of the trusses on the Petrel.

"Zeke, drop the cases. Try to land on your feet. Push off! Push off!"

"I thinnnnkkk I am going to be siiick," Zeke said.

Jake watched, helpless, as Zeke spun toward Nadine on the Petrel. Suzanne was yelling something over the channel, but he couldn't understand. He was focused on his friend spinning in space, out of control.

He leaped out of the airlock, trained right on where Zeke was spinning. But the ship rolled and he lost sight of Zeke.

"Zeke!" Jake yelled as he landed on the side of the Petrel.

A sealed case banged around the edge of a truss and floated to a halt. Jake bounded around the corner, and saw Zeke caught up around a truss, floating. He wasn't moving, and his back looked the wrong shape. There wasn't any armor in a regular skinsuit, nor any fancy body monitoring tools, and Zeke wasn't answering his radio. Jake jumped up, rolled Zeke toward him, and touched helmets.

"Zeke, are you okay?"

Zeke grimaced up at Jake through his helmet. He looked to be in pain. Then he smiled.

"Zeke, you'll be fine. We'll get you inside and put you in a med computer."

"I do not think that will help. I— I cannot move my legs. I feel very cold."

"I'll just move you around here, Zeke. Stay focused."

"You have been a good friend, Jake."

"Just hold on, Zeke," Jake said as he held onto Zeke with one arm and pulled himself along the Petrel with his other.

"That was a pretty impressive jump. Do you not think so?"

"It was great, Zeke. You did great."

"I . . . I hope Nadine saw it."

"She did."

"Good. I wonder if she has a boyfriend? She would be fun."

"Sure, Zeke. Why don't you ask her when we get inside?"

But Zeke did not answer back.

16

Suzanne was yelling over the comm as Nadine came around the truss to help. They took Zeke and steered him around and into the airlock. Nadine paused to grab his two cases and stuff them in the airlock as well. Jake had Suzanne wait at the airlock as Colau, who was too scared to jump, came down the line hand over hand. Jake and Nadine carried Zeke toward the med bay.

"Shit," Jake said.

"It looks like he broke his back," Nadine said. "He must have hit something."

They were lucky that the medical unit was on the same deck. They hurtled around the corner and loaded Zeke up, then slammed the lid down. The machine began to flash codes. First green, then yellow, then red. Probes extended from the inside and touched his head and chest. Displays on the machine stayed red. Words finally formed. "No response."

The door behind them opened, and Suzanne and Colau came in.

"Zeke, are you okay? Zeke. Jake, what happened?" Suzanne stopped when she got next to the medical unit and looked at the displays. Then she turned to Nadine. Nadine didn't say anything, just shook her head.

"Suzanne, I'm sorry. He's dead. He broke his back when he hit the ship. It . . . it killed him."

"His heart stopped. Shouldn't it be shocking him? Like in the vids?"

Jake shook his head. "There are no brainwaves. It won't bring his heart back if his brain has stopped working."

Suzanne didn't speak. She just started bawling. Jake felt like bawling himself. He sat down. Nadine patted them both on the shoulder, then headed off with Colau in tow. "I'm going to find the bridge and start getting us out of here."

Nadine hustled through the Petrel to the bridge. There was no one on board. They must have abandoned ship after they had hooked up the tow lines to the Onion. Life support and power was on but at a caretaker level. It was a bit cold and dark, and she could tell that the air pressure was lower than normal.

The staterooms were empty. The airlock to the bridge was wide open, and the control board wasn't even locked down. She tapped a few screens and started a checklist to bring the engine online. The engine board showed green. Somebody must have repaired the control lines, she thought.

She brought the engines up to standby and remotely released the cable holding them to the Bountiful Onion. To her surprise, it worked and they were free. She hunted for the speaker controls.

"Everybody, we're dropping. Low-G first, but be ready." Nadine keyed a very gentle .1 G thrust, and they began to creep away from the Onion.

Something flashed right in front of the control room. Nadine raised her eyebrows and keyed the speaker again.

"Jake, get up here. I need you."

Jake must have already been on his way, because it was only a matter of seconds before he came through the door behind her.

"What's up?"

"Somebody's alive on the Bountiful Onion's bridge. And they're shooting at us."

***

"But, sir, I told you. We're not pirates. And we certainly didn't kill your crew. That was the disease." Jake had managed to contact the Bountiful Onion. The captain and a single rating were still alive. The rating was on the bridge, linking the captain's internal comm with the external one to Jake. The rating was also, at the captain's order, firing the laser at them. But he must have been uncomfortable with bridge operations because he appeared to have no idea how to adjust the targeting computer. His shots were wide. Jake began to understand how they could have dumped both the fuel and the reaction mass by accident.

"Liar." The captain's voice rang over the comm. "All my crew are dead! And they all got sick from your ship. Why aren't you sick? Why are you immune and not my crew?"

"I've been immunized."

"And why were you immunized against this specific disease? It was so you could infect us and then steal from us and escape unharmed, wasn't it, pirate!"

"I told you. It happened where I lived, when I was a child. Either way, sir, most of my crew died as well. Enough about that, though. Sir, you're on a collision course with an asteroid. You need to get off the ship and come with us."

"This is a TGI pirate plot to steal the Bountiful Onion. You're just waiting until we all die and then you'll seize the ship. That is why you ran away, to call to your pirate friends to come and pick us up."

"Sir, we ran away because we didn't want to crash into the asteroid!"

"Or freeze to death," Nadine added. She was able to control her board one-handed, for the most part. But she wasn't going to be doing any fancy flying.

Jake shook his head at her and turned back to the speaker. "Could you please stop shooting at us, sir?"

The captain continued yelling at them, and then began yelling at the rating on the bridge to keep firing. A pale-faced Suzanne entered the bridge and sat down. "What's going on?" she asked.

"Well, according to Colau over there," Jake said, pointing at Colau, who was sitting in the corner of the bridge, "we're hearing Captain Crazy over there, who's locked in his stateroom. The guy on the bridge doesn't seem to know what he's doing, but the captain has him running things. They're currently shooting at us because the captain still thinks we're pirates and he won't believe me that they're about to hit an asteroid."

"Jake," Nadine said from the control board, "their maneuvering jets just fired. Big energy surge over there."

"I thought that they had no power?"

"They don't. Ah, shit. It's the mass driver. They're firing from the capacitors."

"Well, what do we do now?" Suzanne said. She didn't sound that interested in the answer.

"We zig and zag, and hope they run out of power before we run out of time."

"What happens if they hit us?" Suzanne asked.

"We'll die."

"Fire again, idiot," Captain Marchello screamed. "They're pirates. If we don't kill them, they'll seize the ship."

"Sir, I'm trying, but I'm not very good at this."

"Silence! You are a trained member of this crew. That is why you are here."

"I'm here because your cousin yanked me out of a sweet gig at that five-star spa. I've never fired a mass driver," he yelled over the comm. "I'm just your masseuse!"

"Keep firing. Go to rapid fire. Fast as you can."

"Yes . . . yes, sir." He looked down and found a button for mass fire. Well, at least he could do that right.

The mass driver began to dump steel cubes into the track, and a group of electromagnets began to propel them down at supersonic speeds. It was a very delicate balance—the metal cube started at rest, was magnetized by the first magnet, and then the computer switched on a magnet slightly behind that that "pushed" the cube forward, then another magnet re-magnetized the cube, then another pushed the cube faster and farther, and the process repeated until the cube came screaming out the front.

This relied on very precise measurements of the magnetic fields, as well as a very stiff sub-structure holding everything together.

The Bountiful Onion was a very old ship. It still flew, but repairs had been made over the years with different materials. Expansion and contraction in space and good old-fashioned metal fatigue had taken its toll. As the mass driver went to rapid fire, the ship was still spinning, trying to get the Petrel on target.

The hull flexed. Just a little.

"Wow!" Nadine yelled. Jake had pointed a telescope at the Onion and put it on screen, so Nadine could tailor her random course changes to keep making things difficult. They watched the Bountiful Onion as a series of explosions burst just below the crew decks and the front of the ship blew off.

"Jake, what did you fire at them?" Nadine asked.

"Nothing. It wasn't us," he said, wide-eyed.

"They just did the ship equivalent of shooting themselves in the foot." Nadine laughed.

"Pretty spectacular screw-up," Jake said.

"Good. They killed Zeke. I want them to die," Suzanne said.

Nadine and Jake looked at each other but didn't say anything.

"Jake, can you get us a course back to the Roundhouse? That's the nearest station."

"Yes, Let me program it in."

"Good, because that shot is starting to wear off, and my arm is hurting like hell."

"Give me a minute and I'll have it. Once it's locked in, why don't you all go and get some sleep. We'll need a bridge watch, so I'll take first shift. It will take us about seventeen hours to get to the station. You two need some rest."

"I'm up for that," Nadine said.

In short order, Nadine had locked in the course, and bounded off the bridge toward one of the staterooms. Suzanne and Colau left as well. Jake sat down and turned all the passive sensors on, and all the monitoring systems on. He didn't want to be surprised again. He did notice a spike in power as Nadine sent a very large, very loud electronic message, but it was encrypted, and he didn't really care that much. He waited an hour until he was sure both of them were asleep and went back to the med bay. Zeke's body was still there, and he had a lot of work to do.

Eight hours later he returned to the bridge. His body was as tired as it had ever been, and he felt mentally drained. His arms ached and so did his back. He buzzed the cabins to wake the girls.

Suzanne came up first. "You look beat, Jake."

"I am. Suzanne, I've cleaned up Zeke's body and dressed him in better clothes. I've got him in a sleep sack and tied to a metal frame. I've figured out a course. If you'd like, I can set it up so that we can eject him so that he floats down into the Dragon, eventually. He'll burn up on re-entry. That's the way we did it at my station."

Suzanne looked very sad for a moment. "That was kind of you, Jake. Yes, let's do that. I have a few things to put with him, and we would always say prayers at home. But he always wanted to go into space, so this will do."

Suzanne collected Nadine. Jake made a few course corrections and told them when to let Zeke go. They watched for a few minutes as Zeke floated into space. Suzanne said some words in Francais. After Zeke was on his way, Jake brought them back on course for the Roundhouse.

Suzanne and Nadine came onto the bridge. Suzanne slumped down in the co-pilot's seat. Jake got up from his seat and turned the helm over to Nadine.

"Nine hours until we arrive. I'm going to get some rest. Wake me up when we're almost there."

Nadine nodded. Jake looked over at Suzanne but she didn't say anything. Jake turned and headed for the nearest cabin. He really did want a long sleep.

***

A long time later, Jake woke feeling bleary. The light in his cabin was on. He checked his comm. Over nine hours. That was long enough. He collected himself and belted on the revolver that he had brought to the cabin. He walked up to the bridge. It was unmanned, purely on auto-pilot. He looked at their course. They had slowed down—it would be another six hours before they got to the Roundhouse at this rate. He flicked through his monitors. Nadine and Suzanne were just coming into the airlock from outside. He flicked to the outside cameras. A very small vessel had matched their velocity off the port airlock. It looked like a ship's launch. Not a lot of range but a great deal of speed. It would have come from another ship close by.

He turned and climbed down the ladders to the airlock. Nadine and Suzanne must have heard him, because they were waiting for him. Nadine had a rifle. That was new. Suzanne carried one of the cases of platinum they had brought over.

"Nadine. Suzanne."

"Jake," Nadine said.

"Where did you get the rifle?"

"From the locker outside. You are wearing a revolver."

"I am. Is that the last of the cases?"

"Yes, the rest are all across. We were going to go up to your cabin to wake you up and then tie you up. But I guess we don't have to now."

"You aren't going to shoot me again, are you, Nadine?"

"Only if I have to. That was just business, Jake. Don't make it personal."

"I won't."

Suzanne turned to Jake. "Jake, give us the gun."

"What if I pull it and try to shoot you, Suzanne?"

"Jake, I've seen you shoot. You missed a standing target at five feet. We are in no danger."

"Is Nadine as good a shot as you with the rifle?"

"Do you want to find out?"

"Not really. I'm going to unbuckle the holster belt and hand it to you. Don't shoot."

Jake unbuckled the gun belt. Suzanne took it.

"Suzanne, are you going with Nadine?"

"Yes, we talked a long time while we were locked up on the Onion and on the bridge after Zeke's . . . after Zeke's funeral. She has a job for me. It sounds interesting. Zeke would have said it was fun." Suzanne teared up a bit.

"The Militia will be looking for you. Technically, we're still indentured to them."

"Nadine seems to think we can avoid them. And what do I care?" Suzanne gave her patented shrug. "Zeke is dead. Besides, it will be an adventure."

"Zeke would have been proud."

"Yes, I think he would have been."

"I assume that, after you leave, I'll go back to the bridge and find that the console is locked or that you've cut maneuvering or something."

"We dumped a lot of fuel. You'll be able to make Roundhouse but only if you stay on this course," Nadine said.

"Did you kill Colau?"

"No. Just gave him some basic laced with sleeping pills we found in the med bay. He should sleep for a day."

"Well, thanks for not killing him. Or me."

"Jake, we would not have killed you," Suzanne said. "I like you too much."

"We aren't going to have any problems with you, are we?" Nadine asked.

"How? I don't have much fuel. And I'm sure the weapons are down too."

Nadine nodded her head.

"Honestly, I'm not even going to turn on the sensors to track you. I'll say that you disabled those and that I managed to fix them later. You're free and clear."

"Aren't you mad about the PMGs?"

"It's not like they're mine, Nadine. And you do have a gun."

"Do you want to come with us?" Suzanne asked.

"Yeah," Nadine said. "Suzanne here says you aren't nearly as useless as I always thought. The people I work for might be interested in having you around."

"Yes, Jake. Come with us," Suzanne said.

Jake stood and thought about it for a very long time.

"No. I think I'll stay here."

Suzanne looked disappointed. Nadine looked smug. "Told ya," she said, turning to Suzanne. "You owe me ten credits." She turned back to Jake. "Jake, I like you, so I want to tell you something."

"Yes?"

"You're a horrible spy. You should get out of this business. You're just not fit for it."

"Why do you say that?"

"You think too much. You can't shoot. You're useless in any sort of physical situation. You tend to panic."

Jake stared at her. "Well, I like to think I have other skills."

"You do, but they aren't any good in this business. You're out of your league, Jake."

"I'll try to remember that."

"And the most important thing, Jake."

"Yes?"

"You always lose." Nadine smiled. "Goodbye, Jake," she said, and turned and walked into the airlock.

"Goodbye, ladies. Free trades."

"Free trades," Nadine said over her shoulder.

Suzanne smiled at him again. Jake looked over her shoulder to see Nadine fussing with the airlock control. He stepped forward, pulled Suzanne by her shoulders, and gave her a passionate kiss full on her lips. She leaned right into it and kissed him back. Jake stopped and stepped back. He looked at Suzanne. "I should have done that a long time ago."

"Yes, Jake. You should have." She arched her eyebrows and stuck her tongue out at him. "Goodbye, mon cheri. Say hello to Mr. D for me," she said, following Nadine into the airlock, pulling it closed.

Jake looked at the closed airlock door. Say hello to Mr. D? Surely she didn't mean Mr. Dashi? How would she know him? Did she mean Nadine's crewman Big D? He shook his head. He was tired and that felt too complicated right now.

Jake turned around and trudged up to the bridge. As promised, his fuel situation was not quite critical but close enough. He set up a conservative cruising course and checked that all the systems were green, at least as many as he could. He set up the passive sensors and a telescope to monitor the launch as it blasted away. It was doing at least 4 G—no way would he ever catch it. He thought about going out to fix whatever they had done to the laser and antennas. They had probably just unplugged the control runs again. But it might be misinterpreted if he went out on the hull right now. They could be watching him with a telescope, and that craft might be armed. Instead, he just got a cup of basic and sat in the captain's chair and pondered his career choices.

***

After four hours the launch coasted up to a small station. "Do we owe you anything?" Nadine asked their pilot.

"Nope, all taken care of. Your ride is across the bay. Go quickly. There is a pretty narrow launch window for where you want to go."

Nadine and Suzanne grabbed the cases and hauled them across the deck to the other ship. Suzanne managed four, two per arm, and Nadine two in her unbroken hand. The cases were more awkward than heavy and felt lighter in the station's gravity than Suzanne had expected.

As soon as they entered the next ship, a long-distance speeder, the crew closed the airlock and began to drop. The cargo master was right there and made them each stand on a scale to get an exact mass. It was a very narrow window, and they had to hit it just right.

"Two girls and twenty-eight kilograms of metal cases," he announced.

Nadine looked up. "Your scale must be off. That should be about 150 kilograms of metal cases."

"Nope, twenty-eight."

"Are you sure? Could your scale be wrong?"

"You and your clothes and that gun's combined mass is exactly seventy kilograms. That sound about right?"

"Yes."

"The scale isn't off."

Suzanne looked at Nadine. Nadine opened one of the cases and looked at the small metal bars on the top. She hefted one of them, then another, then began pulling them out. She stopped when she pulled out one in the second layer and weighed it in her hand. It was still a metallic silver, but looked a bit different, less lustrous, than the others. She handed two bars to Suzanne. "Feel these."

Suzanne weighed them in her hands. "This one is heavier."

Nadine nodded. "Hey," she yelled to the cargo master. "Can you tell the difference between platinum and other metals?"

"Sure can, I was a miner for years."

"Tell me about these two." She handed both bars to him. He weighed them in his hands.

"This one is a lot heavier than the other one, but the same color."

"Right."

"It's probably platinum."

"What's platinum worth?"

"Eight hundred credits a kilo."

"What's the other one, then?"

"It weighs about a tenth of the other."

"Seems that way."

"It's probably aluminum. That's eight hundred credits a ton, if you are interested."

Suzanne started to laugh.

Jake watched the stars for a while and then walked back to the galley. He took another cup of basic and walked to the empty stateroom next to his. Piled on the bed were hundreds of ingots of platinum and palladium. In the drawer next to the bed were dozens of ruthenium and rhodium. He'd have to carry them back to the cargo hold and put them in cases before he got to Roundhouse station. He sighed and got to work.

17

"Are these navigation directions correct?" Mr. Dashi asked.

"As far as I can tell, sir," Jake said. He was sitting on the fabric-covered chair in front of Mr. Dashi's enormous wooden desk. He was wearing a clean TGI uniform without any rank insignia, but with a single company flash. His other flashes were all white with black borders—no corporate allegiance. To the casual observer, he was a junior worker hired on contract to TGI.

"Will you be able to find Nadine's ship, then?"

"I can find where it went, sir. Anybody can who follows this orbit. But that's only if it's still there. Somebody else could have calculated this orbit and picked it up already."

"Do you think Nadine has retrieved her ship already?"

"Probably, sir. But we can't be sure."

"Very well. I'll arrange with one of our sub-contractors to rendezvous with this orbit. It's a slim chance that it's still there, but it's worth the opportunity to pick up a functioning ship."

"Yes sir."

"Very good job on your metal retrieval. We have done exceptionally well in the spot market since you brought your cargo back home."

"Yes sir."

Mr. Dashi flipped a few pages on his screen, then closed it down. He turned to look at Jake.

"It's a great tragedy that the entire crew of the Petrel, except for you, died, Jake."

"Yes sir."

"Mr. Vidal and the captain left pretty extensive logs that we were able to recover. Mr. Vidal in particular was quite approving of your actions toward the end."

"We checked the records—there hasn't been a measles outbreak in close orbit since we made landfall."

"Since landfall, sir? You mean since the Delta colony was founded?"

"That's correct—hundreds of years ago. Our doctors didn't realize that it still existed."

"We had it on our station when I was child, sir. That's what my mom told me. Or something like it. I was too young to know for sure. It was very bad. Many people died. After that, I guess I was immune."

"You're very lucky. Since the Onion was destroyed there's no record of how the disease might have been brought on board."

"Nadine thought one of her crewmen had brought it. She mentioned that she had been coughing and feverish before the Onion took us. I wonder where they caught it from?"

"We'll never know, unless we get their log. Another reason to try to match orbit with that ship. But it's not a terrible problem. We have a vaccine—we just stopped using it over a hundred years ago. The inter-corporation medical council has added it back into the required vaccines now, so an outbreak shouldn't happen again."

"That's good, sir."

Mr. Dashi was silent for a moment. Jake sat in silence

as well.

"Congratulations on a job well done, Mr. Stewart. You've redeemed yourself. We'll forget that little problem at the bar before you shipped out."

"That's great, sir. What about the other things Mr. Vidal complained about? The weapons and the shooting?"

"What shooting?" Mr. Dashi sounded puzzled.

"The shooting on the Petrel?"

"I don't know what you're talking about. Mr. Vidal didn't report anything. Was there a shooting on the Petrel?"

Jake nodded. "More of an accidental weapons discharge, sir."

"Mr. Vidal didn't mention anything in his official report."

"He didn't?"

"No. He must not have thought it important enough to mention, Mr. Stewart."

"I see."

"Do you think you should report it to me?"

"I'm not sure, sir."

"Why would you report something that Mr. Vidal didn't think was important? And if it showed Mr. Vidal in a bad light, well, it's too late now. He's dead."

"Yes sir." Jake paused. Mr. Dashi didn't say anything at all, just stared at Jake with his usual enigmatic smile. Jake nodded, swallowed, and continued on.

"We've put your pay into your account, the usual end-of-cruise bonus. Oh, and Jose has a credit chip for all the currency you left in your cabin."

"Sir?"

"All those coins and GG credits in your cabin, along with the excess metal. Mr. Vidal kept careful notes of your trading. We've recovered all the metal that he accounts for. So, the excess must have been your personal property. In the interest of security, we sold it with the others and converted the credits for you. We had to use less than market rate, I'm sorry to report. I'm sure you could have done better, but those are the rules. It's still a very substantial amount. You'll be able to buy a new skinsuit, that's for sure."

"I see." And Jake did see. Vidal must have doctored the records. The unaccounted metal would have gone into his pocket.

"There are often accounting irregularities on these types of missions, Mr. Stewart, given the somewhat slapdash nature of the trading operations. It wouldn't do for regular activities, of course, but for these special operations a little discrepancy is expected. As long as it's reasonable, we just write it off as a cost of doing business."

Mr. Dashi thumbed something on his comm. "There we go. You're on leave for the next two weeks. Report back to Jose fourteen days from now at nine hundred hours. We'll have your next assignment for you. I'd like to see you get into gunnery school, perhaps. I think that would be a useful skill for you to have. Perhaps pilot school. Oh, and I think a technical school. Think you could pass electronics technician?"

"Yes sir, with some time to study."

"Well, you're good at that. Thank you, Mr. Stewart."

Jake realized that the interview was over. He stood up, thanked Mr. Dashi, and left.

Mr. Dashi spun his chair around to look at the painting on his side wall. It was a stylized representation of Delta, Sigma Draconis, and the rings. He regarded it for a few minutes, then pressed his comm button.

"Jose?"

"Sir?"

"Has Mr. Stewart left?"

"Yes sir. With his credit chip."

"Good. I hope he goes shopping."

"Yes sir."

"File the logs from the Petrel as approved. Post Vidal's report to the database with the amendments that I made regarding Jake. Then destroy the private communications from Vidal."

"All of them, sir? Even the special notes about Jake?"

"Yes. Vidal didn't see the whole picture. Things are proceeding as I expected."

"He was pretty critical, sir."

"Critical of the wrong things. Mr. Stewart is not a gunman or a thug, or, for that matter, an analyst. He has different skills."

"Approve log, post report, destroy personal correspondence. Got it, sir."

"Thank you, Jose. You can go after that."

Mr. Dashi swiveled his chair to stare at the painting again. He sat for a long time in the dark. At last, he spoke out loud.

"How did a colony world that has been isolated for eighty-plus years catch a disease that had been eradicated before humans even came here?"

The painting didn't answer.

AUTHOR'S NOTE – GET A FREE EBOOK

Thanks for reading. I hope you enjoyed it. Word-of-mouth reviews are critical to independent authors. Please consider leaving a review on Amazon or Goodreads or wherever you purchased this book.

If you'd like to be notified of future releases, please join my mailing list.

https://dl.bookfunnel.com/utkw99vv1s

I send a few updates a year, and if you subscribe you get a free ebook copy of Sigma Draconis IV, a short novella in the Jake Stewart universe. For release notifications, you can also follow me on Amazon, Bookbub and Goodreads.

Andrew Moriarty

BOOKS BY ANDREW MORIARTY

Adventures of a Jump Space Accountant

1.   Trans Galactic Insurance

2.   Orbital Claims Adjustor

3.   Third Moon Chemicals

4.   A Corporate Coup

ABOUT THE AUTHOR

Andrew Moriarty has been reading science fiction his whole life, and he always wondered about the stories he read. How did they ever pay the mortgage for that spaceship? Why doesn't it ever need to be refueled? What would happen if it broke, but the parts were backordered for weeks? And why doesn't anybody ever have to charge sales tax? Despairing on finding the answers to these questions, he decided to write a book about how spaceships would function in the real world. Ships need fuel, fuel costs money, and the accountants run everything.

He was born in Canada, and has lived in Toronto, Vancouver, Los Angeles, Germany, and Maastricht. Previously he worked as a telephone newspaper subscriptions salesman, a pizza delivery driver, a wedding disc jockey, and a technology trainer. Unfortunately, he also spent a great deal of time in the IT industry, designing networks and configuring routers and switches. Along the way, he picked up an ex-spy with a predilection for French champagne, and a whippet with a murderous possessiveness for tennis balls. They live together in Brooklyn.

Please buy his books. Tennis balls are expensive.

IF YOU ENJOYED THIS BOOK, CHECK OUT THIS EXCERPT FROM 'THIRD MOON CHEMICALS', THE FURTHER ADVENTURES OF JAKE STEWART, JUMP SPACE ACCOUNTANT.

AVAILABLE ON AMAZON.

17

☐ "What's our status?" Jake asked.

"We are tumbling through space, and our main engines are out. One thruster is locked on, forcing a clockwise roll. The roll is increasing steadily, and will soon hit 2 G or above," Riley said.

"Life support?"

"Life support is offline. Breathable air for about thirty minutes until CO_2 causes unconsciousness. There is a small fire in the engine room. One engineering airlock hatch is open to space. Uncertain why."

Jake frowned at the screen in front of him. Stop the roll first. But before he did that—what was ahead of him?

"What's our course?"

"We are tumbling toward a group of asteroids ahead. We may impact them, we may not. Unsure. Details on your pilot's console," Riley said.

Jake looked at his console. Stop the roll first, or change course? How far away were they from the asteroids? Not that far. But the roll kept increasing—if he didn't fix it quickly, they would be pinned in their seats by centrifugal force.

"Firing thrusters two and five." Jake toggled the power. The roll stopped increasing, then began to rapidly decrease. Too fast. He dropped the power of the thrusters until the roll was barely decreasing. Time enough to fix it later.

Now fix the pitch. He fired a combo of thrusters again, and the pitching slowed. He slowly spun the ship so that it was pointing roughly in their direction of travel, rolling slowly with a bit of yaw. Now, get out of the way of the upcoming asteroids, or deal with the fire.

"Main engine?" Jake asked.

"Still offline. No response from engineering on repairs," Riley said. "Fire in engineering increasing. Should

I vent the atmo?"

"What about the crew back there?"

"They report being trapped behind the fire."

"Are they in skinsuits?"

"Not all of them."

The collision alarm bonged again. They were pointed right at the asteroids ahead, and they rolled slowly in a full circle perhaps once every twenty seconds.

The fuel button lit on his screen. Jake smelled hot plastic. Then he saw smoke. Crap.

What now, Jake Stewart?

No main engine. And fuel was leaking out the damaged line. But it wouldn't be leaking in a perfectly coordinated direction. Unless he had some enormously bad luck, it was giving some sort of vector, in some direction.

He just had to figure out what direction.

The collision gong bonged again.

"Time to impact?"

"Computer says two minutes on this course," Riley said. Sweat was starting to run down her face, and her long red hair had become unscrewed from her bun.

"Right. Firing four and five." Jake stabbed buttons on his screen. He eyed the fuel consumption. The pitch stopped completely. The yaw stopped completely. They were floating dead in space. The roll was burning fuel, as was the thruster that was firing against it. But the roll wouldn't be totally neutral. There would be some other vector. He waited.

They were moving backwards.

Backwards didn't matter. What mattered was that they generated a vector at 90 degrees to their current course, so that they would miss the upcoming asteroids.

"How long to impact?"

"One minute. Jake, the fire in engineering is spreading. We need to vent atmo."

Jake looked at her in surprise. "We'll kill them all back there."

"If thruster control goes, we'll lose the whole ship," Riley said. The hot plastic smell was much stronger now, and the sweat was starting to pour down her face. The collision alarm bonged again. The smoke was thickening now. Jake could see it. He coughed once.

The fuel light started flashing. Jake killed the thrusters that were canceling the roll. Without the offsetting counter-thruster, the leaking fuel caused them to start rolling faster and faster. Jake felt himself slide to one side of his seat as the roll began to increase. It was approaching a 2-G roll. He wanted to stop it, but he needed the fuel to spill out to give him the necessary variance in their course to avoid crashing into an asteroid. Canceling the roll would just make their last few moments comfortable until they smashed themselves silly on a rock.

"Thirty seconds."

"Will we clear it?"

"Not yet. A few more seconds."

Jake slid into one side of his chair and felt himself straining against the straps that held him on the seat. Their spin passed 3 G and was on its way to four. Jake felt himself pressed into the corner of his seat. He loaded up the roll and began typing a series of commands onto the screen. But he kept his hands away from the execute button. He set up a counter-thrust to stop the roll.

"Fifteen seconds."

"Will we clear?" Jake said, glancing to the side.

"Uncertain," Riley said. She sounded cool, relaxed, with no emotion at all. But her face was plastered with sweat. "We'll know shortly."

Jake felt like he should be afraid, but the pressure on his seat and on his arms pushed that away. He had a splitting headache, his knees hurt from where they were crammed together, and he could barely move his hands. His vision began to go. He pushed his arm out to the console in front of him. He couldn't quite reach it. He strained as hard as he could. The roll was still increasing—

it would hit 5 G soon and he wouldn't be able to move at all. He pushed as hard as he could, and felt his hands reach the console. He tried to pulse his finger up and down, but he couldn't do it. His finger was locked on the screen. He needed to stop the roll.

His vision was rimmed with black. It was like he was looking down a tunnel that was slowly darkening. He couldn't see his hands at all, just what was in front of him. With a convulsive heave he threw his hands up as high as he could and let them flop back down. It was probably a quarter inch, but it was enough. His descending finger hit the 'engage' button.

The pre-programmed counter-roll thruster fired at full throttle. The rolling stopped increasing, and then began to slowly slow, then more rapidly slow. Jake had programmed it to dump maximum thrust out right from the start. He needed that roll to be cancelled.

"Jake, the fire has reached the fuel lines, next to the damaged airlock," Riley said. "It will—"

BANG.

Jake felt a whoosh as air and smoke began to stream out of the cabin. The explosion must have blown the airlock open and the ship was venting. He would pass out from lack of oxygen in about thirty seconds. He tried to reach up to close his helmet, but his arm couldn't move. The roll was increasing again, and he couldn't pry his hand off the arm. The control runs to the thrusters must be severed.

I wonder which will knock me out first, Jake thought. The increasing G-spin or the lack of air?

He was still trying to decide which it was when he passed out.

Made in the USA
Las Vegas, NV
17 September 2021

30510702R00142